A DREAMER'S
LOG CABIN

A WOMAN'S WALDEN

A DREAMER'S LOG CABIN

BY LAURIE SHEPHERD

DEMBNER BOOKS / NEW YORK

Dembner Books
Published by Red Dembner Enterprises Corp.
1841 Broadway, New York, N.Y. 10023
Distributed by W. W. Norton & Company, Inc.
500 Fifth Avenue, New York, N.Y. 10110

Library of Congress Cataloging in Publication Data

Shepherd, Laurie.
    A dreamer's log cabin.
      1. Log cabins—design and construction.   I.   Title.
TH4840.S48   694   81-3215
ISBN 0-934878-06-4 (pbk.)   AACR2

To my Mother,
who loves me anyway,
and
to Donna Aske,
a good carpenter
and a good friend.

Contents

PART ONE

THE JOURNAL:

A DREAMER'S LOG CABIN

PART TWO

THE FIRST WINTER:

REFLECTIONS IN THE SNOW 133

Introduction:
A Dream Takes Shape

I have always been a dreamer. Most of my dreams flash through my mind, entertain me for a moment, then leave as quickly as they came. But one dream lingered, lodged in my heart, and expanded until it became too important to remain a dream.

My log cabin dream.

It had been growing for twenty years until I could almost hear a voice saying, "Work on me, Laurie. Make me happen."

All dreams start somewhere, and as I look back, I can see how the seeds of my dream were planted and nourished by my childhood experiences.

When I was four years old, my mother and father fulfilled a dream of theirs by moving from our post-war tract home — the typical three-bedroom rambler on a flat, treeless lot — to a larger, two-level house in a more affluent community, nine miles west of Minneapolis. It was the conventional dream of the 1950's: a nice house in the suburbs, with good schools and compatible neighbors close by.

The homesite they chose was a large, triangular lot at the end of a cul-de-sac. Our dead-end street wound past two ponds, and the area — called Sherwood Forest — was filled with mature hardwoods.

This new environment was the scene of childhood adventures that I recall as vividly as though they happened yesterday.

> 1954: We just moved to the forest. There are deer and foxes and raccoons. I have an inner-tube swing, and can climb the rope to the top of a giant tree. I like to watch Daddy build things.

11

1955: Carpenters are building new houses in the woods. When they leave, I tip over the nails and boards. I hope they give up and don't come back. Maybe the trees they cut down will grow again.

1956: Mom made me wear a ruffly dress for Beth's birthday party. I hated the dress. I didn't go. I hid the present in the woods, climbed up a tree, and hid till the party was over. When my brothers found the present, I was in trouble.

1958: I'm an Indian. Doria and I go to the sandpit in shirts we beaded, and play Apache scouts. In school I read all the books about Indians. The librarian helped me find them. I wrote a play about some pioneer children at Thanksgiving time. Some friends acted in it for the class.

1960: I'm Huckleberry Finn. Gail is Tom Sawyer. We built a raft on her pond, and a neat treehouse. The studs are sixteen inches on center. In September a teacher asked if my shoes were too tight because I walk funny. My shoes feel too tight because I went barefoot all summer. She made me walk around the cafeteria during lunch to practice being graceful. I think she walks funny too.

I now am both amazed and grateful that my parents encouraged me in my adventures. While most girls were playing house and jumping rope in the accepted fifties tradition, I was having a grand time in the woods being an Indian, Huck Finn, a pioneer, Robin Hood and Peter Pan. But why not? I always felt I could be anything I wanted to be. While I may have raised a few eyebrows among friends, neighbors and teachers, my family accepted my unorthodox ambitions.

When I announced that I wanted to work in a filling station, my father built me a wooden gas pump with hose attached, so I could pretend to "fill it up." When I decided I'd like to be a tightrope walker, he tied a sturdy rope between two trees so I could practice. It was only three feet off the ground, but I pretended it was a hundred. (My grandmother almost had a heart attack when

my seventy-five-year-old grandfather came outside to try walking the tightrope with me. In spite of a distinguished career as a judge, he must have been a dreamer, too.)

My father, somewhat reluctantly, because he was not a rugged outdoorsman, also introduced me to the wilderness area of northern Minnesota. Another special memory:

> 1961: Father and my brother Jamie and I went to the Boundary Waters canoeing. We camped by a waterfall and stayed until three bears ate up all our food. I've got to go back to that place sometime.
>
> In the fall we started reading a book that is all about a pioneer family in Minnesota. I wish I could have been born a hundred years ago so I could build a log cabin like the one in the book.

Childhood dreams are sometimes pushed aside by new and different adolescent dreams. But I continued my love affair with the North Woods.

As a teen-ager, I attended the Minnesota Outward Bound School. The final seventeen days of the course were spent canoeing with ten other girls through the Quetico, in Ontario, culminating in three days of solitude. The experience had a deep impact on me, and it was a culture shock to return to the easy, short-order style of suburbia. God's world is so astonishing where the human race hasn't scribbled on it.

From adolescence to adulthood, I existed in two worlds. In the real world, I went to the university, drove a school bus to earn my tuition, and eventually became a teacher in Wabasha, a small town in southern Minnesota.

In my dream world, I was back in northern Minnesota building a log cabin.

In addition to teaching art, I taught a six-week rock-climbing and orienteering course — which gave me more satisfaction than the whole year of teaching art. For several years, I took groups of students to northern Minnesota's Boundary Waters Canoe Area, for the joy of sharing it with people who had never experienced it. It was always great fun, but I noticed each time how excited the kids were to see the end of the trip, while I was wishing it wouldn't have to end.

I tried to create my own North Woods environment near the school where I taught, by buying a little house on the Mississippi, just south of Wabasha. It had a fireplace and a loft, and the rustic interior looked somewhat like the numerous log cabins I had designed on paper, but to my chagrin, it was built of studs and siding. My seventy-three-year-old neighbor predicted I'd be living in a log cabin before I turned thirty. Could he have read my dreams?

My friends and family knew me well enough to expect the unexpected, and generally they took my decisions in stride. I always enjoyed seeing the "Now what?" expression on my mother's face when I'd tell her I wanted to have a mother-daughter talk.

In some families that might have preceded an announcement about marriage, or a living-together arrangement, or an unplanned pregnancy. In my case, the announcements were

"I'm going out to North Dakota where someone is going to teach me to drive an eighteen wheeler."

"I'm learning how to tune pianos."

"I'm considering joining the Army Reserves. I could use the extra money and they said I could drive their heavy equipment."

"I want to quit teaching."

"I'm going to learn to be a chimney sweep."

"I've decided to look for some land in northern Minnesota and build a log cabin."

Once I had opted for an early retirement, I turned in my resignation to the school board and took a temporary job as a cook. During this transitional period, I had time to read and write; to sift through my goals and dreams.

I realized my log cabin dream was over. It was time to make it real.

My ticket to building a log cabin was to accumulate a cash fund, enough to buy materials and tide me through the construction period. To produce this fund, I sold my house and worked almost around the clock as an insurance agent, bus driver, dishwasher, janitor, Army Reservist, chimney sweep and piano tuner. Although I felt like a fish out of water, I was beginning to see the lake. But there wasn't much time to dream!

I kept my journal for a year, from October 1978, when I found my land in northern Minnesota, until October 1979, when I moved into my newly built cabin.

This is not intended to be a "how to" account of cabin building. There are many excellent, detailed books on the process — although if you're planning to build, you might be able to gauge your timing more accurately after reading my journal.

The main reason I decided to write down my experiences is because I know many people share a similar dream, or some other equally implausible idea.

If you've ever wanted to "drop out" and live a rustic life in the woods, my journal might inspire you. Or it might jar you into reconsidering.

If anything, I'd rather it made you "drop in." The experiences of working toward a dream can teach you what fun it is to be alive. A dream in the making is an involvement, a risk, a commitment, a joy, a jolt . . . it's a plunge into a mountain stream.

Whatever dream might be in your heart, whether short or long-term, realistic or fantastic, I hope these pages encourage you to go after it.

Sweet dreams. And drop in sometime.

The completed cabin

THE JOURNAL:

PART ONE

A DREAMER'S LOG CABIN

Planning

October 7

I've just looked at four hundred feet of frontage on the Mississippi, not far from its narrow, winding source. Eight acres, high, wooded and beautiful, just what I want.

October 21

I got off work at 9:30 A.M. and drove north from Minneapolis right away to spend a frosty afternoon on my future homesite near Grand Rapids. The underbrush was awfully thick, so I chopped some of it out of the way and tentatively staked out the corners of the cabin. Then I entertained myself for an hour, looking out the "windows," standing at the "sink," and no doubt convincing the local wildlife that there was a lunatic in the woods.

October 28

Mother invited me for lunch and wanted to see the floor plans I've sketched for the cabin, so I brought my notebook along to her comfortable condominium in Minneapolis.

After we ate, I produced a scaled-down outline of a twelve-by-twenty-foot rectangle, and little slips of paper representing the pieces of furniture I'm going to take with me.

Mother rearranged the papers until she came up with a logical,

21

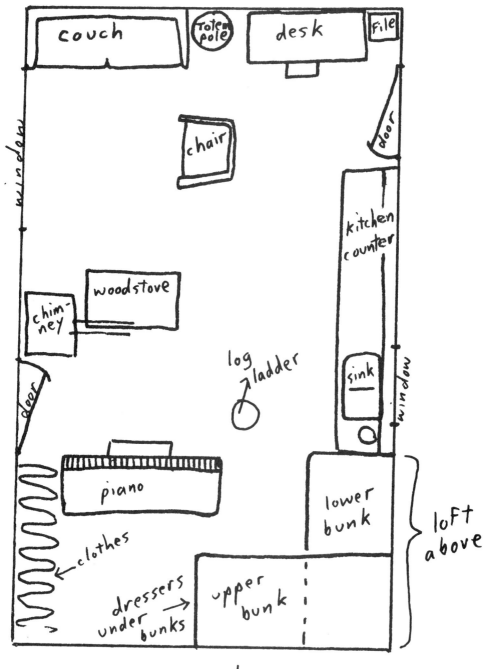

couch

Totem pole

desk

File

window

door

chair

kitchen counter

woodstove

chim-ney

log ladder

window

sink

door

piano

lower bunk

loft above

clothes

dressers under bunks

upper bunk

Floor plan

practical arrangement. It was better than mine, so I drew it to scale and labeled it "Mother's floor plan." Sometimes Mother knows best.

Now all I have to do is eliminate everything I own except the "slips of paper."

November 3

Today I made my last trip to Goodwill and then the dump. As far as I can tell, everything is gone but the things I actually use or wear. And, of course, the sentimental treasures and junk that I'll keep forever.

The dump gave me a strange feeling. People were there scrounging, and one woman started going through the bags I threw off the truck as fast as I could unload them. Even though I was discarding the stuff, I still felt as if she were sorting through my things, and I was irritated by her judgments.

Watching her eyeing some things with interest and casually tossing others on the ground as I stood there, made me want to pack them all back on the truck again. I found out I had more concern for my cast-offs than I had thought possible. But I stuck with my decision to be rid of them, and drove away.

I felt a little annoyed and hostile, but also lighter. Unburdened.

Preparation

November 12

Donna and I met at the property and cleared a trail into my building site with machetes.

> [*Donna is a childhood friend, living in Duluth, who came as often as she could to work with me on the cabin. Without her faithful assistance, I probably would still be peeling logs.*]

November 29

Today I bought the first item for my cabin: a small claw-footed cast-iron bathtub. There was an ad in the paper for thirty-eight of them. I answered the ad and found that the owners of an apartment building in Minneapolis's red light district had redone all the bathrooms and wanted to get rid of the old tubs.

I approached the shabby building and went to Apartment 212 to ask for Harley.

> [*With the exception of Donna and my family, I have changed all the names in this journal. It seemed like a good idea.*]

He showed up at the door in an undershirt and trousers, not entirely zipped and buttoned, and told me the tubs were in the basement. I proceeded down two short flights of dark stairs and through a narrow hall to a dirty room filled with cast-iron tubs and old sinks and toilets. I climbed all over the assortment looking for a tub with no chips in the enamel, and finally (and fortunately) decided on one near the door.

I went back up to see Harley and asked him if he could give me a hand with the tub. He replied that he didn't move tubs, he just sold them. So I asked if there might be someone around who could help. He said, "These winos? Not a chance."

I thanked him and went downstairs again, determined not to leave without a bathtub. Dragging it along the hall wasn't too bad. Pushing and pulling it through the doorway to the stairwell was tough enough. But it was a struggle to inch it up the steep stairway. I groaned, grunted, strained and sweated, and after a half-hour, I reached the first landing.

Looking at the second flight of steps, I realized why bathtubs are now made of fiberglass. With that revelation, I started up the steps again, wondering if my shredded palms would ever grow new skin.

Suddenly a man came down from the first floor, gave me a toothless smile and said, "You need some help?"

With him at the bottom and me at the top, we heaved it up one step at a time. Another man came down and grabbed hold of the tub to help. As the three of us, gasping for breath, finally reached the main floor, I saw Harley and two women peering down at us from the second floor landing. The women wore bright red lipstick and had puffy, tired faces beneath piles of teased hair.

One of my helpers remarked that no one had better mess with me.

We all laughed. I drove my trailer around to the alley door and we loaded the tub. I offered my friends some cash for their help, but they wouldn't accept anything. God bless the winos!

December 25

Some of the tools I'll need for building accumulated under the Christmas tree. Jamie gave me two wedges, a sharpening stone and chain saw blade guard. Mother gave me a hatchet and three pairs of work gloves.

I looked for my double-bladed axe out in the shed, but couldn't find it. Could I have left it in Wabasha by mistake?

Speaking of Wabasha, I told my church youth group what I was going to do. They seemed intrigued, and I told them to feel free to bring their sleeping bags and lend a hand any time, once I started building. They thought that sounded like fun, but I'll believe them when I see them helping.

January 17

I get many different reactions to my plan to build a cabin by myself. Here are some of my favorites:

A lab technician: "Who's going to take care of my insurance?"

An insurance office manager: "It's a waste. How will you pay your debt to society? You're capable of so much more."

An old woman: "How are you going to find a man way up there by yourself?"

An old man: "I'm not surprised. I figured you'd do it pretty soon."

A waitress: "You're really brave."

A teacher: "Are you going to be a hermit?"

Two chimney sweeps: "Good luck."

I deliberately waited until I had a definite moving date before I told anyone what I was going to do. I wasn't in a hurry to have to deal with all the reactions. Generally, I've been able to take them in stride and laugh along with people as they express their surprise and doubt and wonder.

But some reactions do hurt. I don't expect everyone to understand what I'm doing, but it leaves me feeling frustrated and upset when people suggest that I'm dropping out, or being less than I could be, or falling short of my financial potential and hypothetical social commitments. Negative remarks have been few, but those few seem to condemn me for choosing to leave what I believe is an unfulfilling rat race.

My response is to delve into Burns to be reminded that "The man o' independent mind, / He looks and laughs at a' that," and into Thoreau to find reassurance that it's all right to hear a different drummer. I underline sentences I'd like to point out to people who misunderstand my motivation.

February 17

Donna and I drove to my property, chain saw and axes in hand. We got within one-quarter mile of where we would park, and Donna started pulling over. I said she should stay in the middle of the road. Alas, before she could react, we plunged sideways into a drop-off hidden by snow. The car perched perilously at 45 degrees. We climbed out and trudged to the Binners' for rescue. Tom and his sons came right away with their logging skidder. The winch pulled up the LeMans and got it back on the road unharmed. Very lucky. Then we hiked into Binners' woods to see their trees and he said that in a few weeks he would cut enough balsam for me to pick and choose from. Finally, we went — or rather, waded — through waist-deep snow to my building site and managed to fell about ten small trees. In the process, the pull-cord on the chain saw snapped suddenly and almost broke Donna's knuckle. It wasn't Donna's day. We worked until the sun got low and finally headed to Minneapolis.

It occurred to me on the way back to the city how little we had accomplished and how much time had been spent dealing with errors we had made. I can see that I have a lot to learn.

March 19

Complications! Tom Binner didn't cut any trees for me as he promised, so I took the bus to his place for nothing. I called Dave Williams though, and got the names of some other loggers and a back hoe operator.

Then a letter came from Emil Anderson saying that since I was building close to the river I shouldn't put in a basement because the ground is all clay and it heaves and cracks all winter. A heaved basement makes a horrible mental picture.

I just called one of the loggers, who says he's got a pile of Norway pine for me to look at, once he gets it out of the woods. Then Mr. Swain, the back hoe operator, said he'd do my excavation. He said if I backfill around the basement with gravel instead of clay, I shouldn't have a big problem. He lives across the river from me.

I set a date for the phone company to come out and install a phone. The service representative asked if it was going in a house, mobile home, or what. I said I wanted it put on a tree.

"A tree?" she said.

"Yes, a tree."

There was a pause.

"A tree?"

"Well, you see, I'm going to be building a house, and in the meantime, I'd like to have a telephone installed on the tree outside my tent."

"I'll have to speak with my supervisor."

There was another, longer pause, during which I was sure the previous conversation was being repeated word for word to the supervisor. Finally, the woman returned. As she cleared her throat, I visualized Lily Tomlin sitting very erectly at the switchboard.

"A tree will be fine."

She continued asking questions to complete her order form, but I noticed she never asked if I wanted any extensions.

March 22

I went to Carla Wendt's junk shop. She located a bunch of things I need: one scribe, several shovels, two lanterns, a mailbox, and a couple of gasoline cans.

March 31

I officially resigned from all my jobs. Just two weeks left to go! To a dreamer, this suddenly seems very real.

It was an immense relief to know I would leave my jobs in two weeks. The pressure of rushing from one to the other around the clock was getting to be a real strain.

I had reached the point where I was leaving the phone off the hook when I was home so I could get a few hours of undisturbed sleep. It was necessary, but it cut me off from people who wanted to reach me.

Each day I race from job to job, where there are always lots of people, but at the same time, I've never been more isolated. If I didn't have a goal, I'd go crazy. The goal keeps me happy, so I'm able to cope with the chaos and the isolation.

April 10

I closed the sale on my mobile home today. It looks as if the cabin is financed. It had better be — nothing more is coming in. From here on, it's going out.

The night crew at Perkins [restaurant] surprised me with a "scrubwoman" cake and fifteen dollars cash. I'll miss them, but not the work.

The Move

April 16

I moved. Everything isn't out of the trailer yet. It will take a couple of weekends to gather up the final odds and ends and either store them in Mother's garage, or bring them up north.

UP NORTH. Jamie helped me move yesterday. It was a beautiful Easter Sunday, sunny and in the forties. We got to my land at 4:00 P.M. and walked back to where I had planned on setting up my tent. The snow was two feet deep, and the idea of carrying two dressers, a desk, a bed, the tent, and various other essentials through four hundred feet of deep snow didn't seem to appeal to Jamie. Consequently, we set everything up just off the road in the midst of the Binners' farm equipment.

It got quite cold overnight, and it didn't take Lonach and Chisholm long to crawl inside my sleeping bag with me. A little crowded, but warm. I'm afraid if we had all inhaled at once we would have split a seam, but the cats staggered their purring.

The phone man came about 3:00 P.M. He strung the wire one-quarter mile down the road, then overhead betweeen two trees. Finally he hiked back through the woods stringing the wire right to my little phone booth on the tree.

He said he had never had an installation quite like it.

April 19

I got back from town about 3:00 P.M., going by way of Will

Reinhardt's [the logger]. Mr. Reinhardt wasn't home but I talked to his partner. The logs — Norway pine — are lying by the side of the highway and look perfect. I probably can cut each log into two sections, one each for the short and long sides of the cabin. Mr. Reinhardt is supposed to come by and give me a price.

Meanwhile, at the tent, it's 65 degrees outside and about 75 inside, but very windy. Whenever I get this thing back in the woods, I'll tie some rope to the poles and anchor them to some nearby trees for stability. All the snow is gone from the front clearing. Soon it will disappear from the woods.

I finally got to work and dug a proper latrine.

April 26

Donna is babysitting the cats till I can get my tent set up in the woods.

It was a clear, chilly 24 degrees last night, but my double sleeping bags kept me very warm. Now it looks like rain or snow.

I put a down payment on the logs today. Now I can call them mine. There wasn't much else to do, so I took my chain saw and cut up a dead birch tree for firewood.

May 5

Tuesday I called Mr. Swain to see if he could come with his back hoe to dig the hole for my outhouse and cut a road, but he said the ground was still too wet. I just couldn't bear to wait another two or three weeks, so I started digging by myself. Four hours later I was down over my head with just enough strength left to pull myself up and out. That was work! I was so tired I couldn't write until today. Finally, I can stand up from a chair in one smooth, painless movement.

The next day I asked Mr. Binner to cut a rough road to the river for me with his skidder. He hit one low, soggy spot, so I spent the afternoon dragging logs into the deep ruts. My back ached, but

Digging for the outhouse

the logs will provide a solid surface to walk on and eventually drive over.

Thursday Donna showed up to help me move the tent and everything in it to the riverbank. We took most of the day, but what a joy to be camped by the river at last.

May 9

Cold and rain every day, all week. When I see the sun I'm going to rejoice. It took the last two days to get my outhouse built. It sure beats my old latrine hole. I told the Simmons, friends from Wabasha, that my outhouse was near completion, and Jane said, "Gross." That's her perspective. From my perspective, it's my first real luxury.

The conversation reminded me what a difference perspective can make. I mentioned the outhouse because it was my first real accomplishment. I was proud finally to have done something, and it really was an improvement over the temporary latrine, but the Simmons hadn't understood. They seemed to think it was just crude.

I see the importance of looking at someone else's accomplishments from their viewpoint and not my own. Even though I might see no value in something, I'd like to be able to appreciate its meaning for someone else.

May 12

The sun is shining! The temperature is only in the upper thirties, but the sun feels warm. It has been six days since I've bathed, so I decided it was a must before going to Duluth. I put on a tank suit and high-top tennis shoes and headed for the river, with shampoo, soap and thermometer in hand. The water temperture was 45 degrees — plenty cold, but no worse than some mountain streams I've washed in. I completed the scrubbing as fast as possible, then

The outhouse

ran up the hill for a cold shower rinse. Thanks to the sun, it was warm in the tent and I dressed in relative comfort.

May 15

I had a surprise waiting for me when I got home. Just inside the tent was a package of homemade hot cross buns and a note that said, "Welcome. Come and see us. The Andrews, across the river."

I'll paddle across this afternoon or tomorrow.

A second major event was the arrival of my tractor. Now if Will Reinhardt will bring my logs over, I can get to work.

The cats are getting well settled into their pen and cathouse. There's plenty to watch, the sun is warm, and they look pretty content.

I guess that's all they need for contentment: entertainment and warmth. I share the same view and the same sun, but I don't think I share their contentment. I'm too anxious to be building. I want to be peeling logs and building my house, but instead I'm playing a waiting game. Accomplishment has to be part of my contentment.

The Logs Arrive

May 18

Will Reinhardt showed up with my logs. He took two trips. He was full of jokes and wisecracks and appeared to be having a grand time. I had asked him to bring sixteen-foot logs for the ends of the cabin, and twenty-four-foot logs for the two longer sides. Somehow we misunderstood each other, and he cut a few twenty-foot lengths instead of twenty-four-foot lengths. He might have cut all the long ones four feet too short if I hadn't been paying attention. Instead, we laughed about it, and when he brought the second load, the long logs all measured precisely twenty-four feet.

I started working on a boom for moving the logs up on the house. The boom resembles a hydraulic crane made of long narrow logs. It's all set to go, but I need help to raise it into position. When I called Donna, she said Mary Anderson, a friend from Minneapolis, was going to come over tomorrow with two of her friends, Janet and Patti. Another problem solved. They can help!

May 19

I got up at 8:00 A.M. and started arranging my logs to get them all down to one level. It was a lot of work, but I got them organized. I've finished peeling three. There's no law that says I must peel the logs, but I know that if I leave the bark on I'll be sharing my cabin with thousands of delighted insects. I also want the logs to dry out, so the sooner I get them peeled, the better.

May 20

Mary arrived yesterday afternoon with Janet and Patti. Then came the effort. First I went twenty-five feet up Mary's extension ladder. It was so wobbly we tied it to the tree, about in the middle. At the top I tied myself to the tree. The bottom of the boom was braced against the bottom of the tree. Then Mary, Patti and Janet began to raise the tops of the two thirty-foot poles. My friends reached the limit of their strength and energy before they could hoist the poles, so they slowly let them down as I helped by holding the poles back with the cable.

For the second try, I wrapped my end of the cable around the tree for a belay.

[*A belay is rock-climbing technique. One end of a rope is tied around a climber's waist. The other end is passed around the back of a belayer's waist. The belayer controls the slack in the rope so that if the climber falls, the extent of the fall is mini-mized, and the friction of the rope around the belayer's waist creates a braking action. Because of the excessive weight of the boom, I used the tree as the friction point, rather than my waist!*]

The others hoisted the boom in unison, resting between each heave while I held it at that step by belay. By the time the boom was high enough, they were almost six feet from the tree — the worst possible place to gain any leverage. But we got it high enough, and I tied off the end of the cable to hold the boom in place. Now if the thing works, I have the capability of lifting all my logs.

When people skeptically ask me how I'm going to get my logs up, I can quietly reply, "I have a boom."

Lashing braces on the boom

May 22

Drizzle, drizzle, drizzle. It rained all night and now it's going to drizzle all day.

May 23

The day started with beautiful, warm sunshine. Of course it rained again this afternoon which is why I'm sitting here writing instead of being outside working.

Will brought my rafters today, and I paid him for all the logs. It seems incredible that my whole house is lying out by the road, like so many Lincoln Logs, waiting for the children to come and build something out of them.

The rain was brief. It looks as if I can get back to work.

May 29

Donna met me Monday and we peeled four wall logs. Today we raced through all thirty-nine rafter logs. We timed one in four minutes. The bark zipped off like banana peels. It's too bad the Norways don't peel as easily.

I'm suffering from an unexpected agony. For the first time in my life I've picked up poison ivy. My arms are covered with a rash and it is driving me crazy, but I think it's getting better.

May 31

Donna and I peeled five twenty-four-foot logs today in about four hours.

> [*Different types of logs peel differently. Cedar and balsam peel in long strips like bananas, and almost as easily. Once you get a piece started, you can take hold of it with one hand and rip it the whole length with an upward whip of the arm.*

Peeling logs

Norway pine isn't like that, especially if it's been cut when the sap is down. My logs were cut in winter, so the bark was well cemented to the wood. Each log had to be peeled one stroke at a time with a draw-knife. After working down the length of the log, it would have to be rolled, so another strip could be shaved off. It was tedious, hard work, but I liked the irregular coloration. Logs that strip-peel are smooth and white, while the draw-knife will leave behind some of the darker inner bark.]

Last night I called Richard Swain and had a hard time pinning him down on a day he can dig my basement.

It should be next week.

June 1

Dave Williams, a local builder, has agreed to lay the blocks for my basement. He said he'd come out Sunday to stake the basement corners. Today it was cloudy and rainy when I woke up, so I just lay in bed dozing until 11:30 A.M. By then the skies had cleared so I got up and peeled a log. Then I marked and numbered all the logs so I can plan in what order to use them.

June 3

Help! The mosquitoes have come. I think they all hatched at once. They chased me as I carried my ice box from the truck to my tent. Lord, have mercy!

Bruce's wedding was yesterday, so I was gone for the day. [Bruce is Donna's younger brother.] Whenever I'm away from my homesite, I come back to find the greens richer and fuller. The woods smell delicious.

June 4

I'm sitting at my desk by the light of two candle flames. It has been

Donna digs the garden

an exhausting day, but I haven't accomplished so much since I built my outhouse.

Donna and I peeled six twenty-four-footers, which were the last of the long ones. We got done about 3:30 P.M. and then ran two miles. The moment we got back from our run, Mrs. Herder was there waiting for me. She wanted me to come right away and saw my lumber with her and Don. The Herders own a small sawmill a few miles down the road. I'll be seeing quite a bit of them for the next few days.

From 4:00 P.M. until 9:30 P.M. we sawed, and I watched my roof boards, subfloor and porch boards piling up as fast as we could stack them. Tomorrow we'll finish with the main floor joists and whatever else Don can cut out of what's left. There's plenty left for outbuildings. I don't know what he'll charge for all the sawing, but it's pennies compared to what I would have to pay if I was buying all that lumber.

I didn't get home till well after dark. As I walked through the woods I could hear all the creatures who live in the underbrush darting around in response to my footsteps. My clearing was lit by a half moon.

June 5

Donna and I began to turn over my garden with a pitchfork. After a couple of hours of toiling in the sun, we went to town and rented a power tiller. Starting it was harder than working by hand, but once it was running it did the job very efficiently.

I needed a couple of skid logs to lay all my new lumber on, so I hopped on the tractor to go and drag some poplars out of the woods. I accidentally started in fifth rather that first gear, and nearly ran over my peeled logs at full speed.

I instantly recalled Phil Silvers' disastrous tractor ride in the old movie, "Summer Stock." Howling with excitement, I depressed the clutch and stopped before destroying myself or the tractor.

Pets

June 9

Rain. The new garden needs it. Mother and Bob didn't need it. They came for their first visit and were a little repelled by the squishy mud underfoot and wet droplets overhead. Along with them came McKay, a rather thin but lovely Siberian Husky. I am amazed at how much she is managing to walk inside my tent. I think she has covered a half mile by now. From a large house to a tent is certainly a shock for her.

June 10

Today wasn't a day, it was an occasion. I heated water, washed up, put on a DRESS, and went to the nearest church five miles away. After the service, I was invited to dinner by Mrs. Andrews. She probably wanted John to see me dressed up. Finally, before shedding my costume, I went over to my new neighbors, and presented them with a small box of candy. It was time for a friendly gesture.

Back to normal at last, I peeled two logs and did little else. McKay is a little insecure at this stage of her life, so I spent quite a bit of time with her. She learns very quickly and wants to please above all else. After a few jerks on the choke chain she started heeling perfectly. I also taught her to sit and lie down. The problem area is whining when I walk away from her to use the

outhouse or whatever. But she does love to please, so I know she'll be fine.

She certainly has changed the atmosphere around here. Suddenly I have a devoted, demanding dependent, like a five-year-old child. Lonach and Chisholm are being less than cordial. If they growl any louder, they'll probably attract half a dozen bears. But I guess they're entitled to feel a little put out.

June 11

It's that time of year again. I realized the cats were overdue for their rabies and distemper shots, a precaution I always take with them.

The thought of driving thirty miles to a veterinarian with two obnoxious, uncooperative cats struck me as being a real strain to their voices and my nerves. Instead, I left them home, and when I went to town on other business, I talked the vet into giving me the necessary equipment and medication to administer the shots by myself.

Chisholm endured bravely, but a sudden, ill-timed kick from Lonach altered the course of the fourth syringe.

I am now relatively certain I won't be coming down with rabies in the near future.

Chisholm

The Excavation;
The Monsoons

June 12

I went out about 3:00 A.M. to use the outhouse and saw the full moon shining in its brightest glory. All the trees were lit up and the moist path seemed to glisten. What a spectacular night!

At 9:00 A.M. Mrs. Swain called and said work on the basement would begin today. So it has been major day. One well spent. The excavation is progressing, Donna and I finished off the log peeling job, and then we lashed several braces across the boom for added strength. Now I've got the pulley and the tongs in place and ready to go.

Eddie Larson called and says he has a pump for me, so that was good news. Eddie lives with his parents about a mile from my cabin. He's always eager to help in any way. I once mentioned that I was anxious to buy a used water pump, and now he has located an old, disassembled pump and put all the pieces together for me. I feel much happier about the progress around here than I did yesterday.

June 13

I stayed at Jean's last night to give her a brief vacation. [She owns a small country store with an adjoining apartment and doesn't like to go away and leave it unattended.] It felt wonderful to take a shower and eat a whole meal, but I was hot all night. It reminded me how long it has been since I've slept at normal room temperature. Staying at Donna's now and then doesn't really count since her dungeon is rarely warmer than 60 degrees.

Now I've returned home for the day. If Richard levels my driveway tonight, I'll be blessed with a new well tomorrow. No more buckets from the Co-op. On the other hand, if the driveway is rough, the well-driller won't be able to bring in his trucks.

There's nothing to do today and I find myself becoming very aware of the changes on my eight acres. The leaves are full and green, and in place of silence is the constant hum and murmur of insects exploring every dimension of my tent. The birds never stop singing, and as I listen to twigs snapping and leaves stirring beyond my range of vision, I wonder what small creatures are at work providing for new families, or, like me, creating a shelter that will be sound and warm when winter returns.

June 15

I got home from Jean's to a big disappointment. The well drillers left a note saying they couldn't get their truck down my road, and I find myself feeling angry at Richard. He could have told me the road wouldn't be ready. To ease my blue mood, I went out and planted twenty-eight Norway and spruce seedlings.

I went to bed at 10:30 P.M., but had a very strange night. In the present tense, it went like this:

12:30 A.M. — McKay starts sniffing around the tent, then growls by the door. She barks, and won't stop. As long as I'm awake, I decide to put her on her leash and visit the outhouse. I get half way to McKay's run when I hear footsteps just ahead. We go back to the tent. Getting out my flashlight with its failing batteries, I shine it at the mosquito netting and its beacon meets two round, glowing eyeballs, staring right back. The eyes look as big as golf balls, about three inches apart. They gaze into the beam of my flashlight, but I can't make out the shape of the prowler's body. I want it to leave. I rattle my big metal pitcher and yell at it to leave. It doesn't.

I really have to use the outhouse now, but I'm scared because I don't know what this stubborn, immovable creature is. McKay trembles. My flashlight and the two eyes peer at each other. I don't like being spooked, so I decide to go out and face this monster. I walk half way over to it, but it doesn't move. As I stand there, it stares at me. Facing it takes the fright out of me, so I about face and go to the outhouse at last. Back in the tent, I shine my light and meet those steady eyes again. It's 2:30 A.M. I go to bed and wish the sun would hurry up so I could check out the footprints.

June 16

A raccoon! Big, smart, poised, and definitely nothing to tangle with. But more amiable than a hungry wolf or a startled bear. (I hope the bears and wolves will excuse me — I occasionally stumble into a Goldilockian frame of mind.)

Eddie Larson called and offered to help me pick up an old culvert for Richard to bury in my driveway. It weighed a ton, but with his boat trailer and winch, we got it home. I had to leave right away to pick up Toni at the bus stop. [She's another friend from Minneapolis who wants to check out what I'm doing here in the woods.]

A heavy, hard rain began to fall. Home again, Donna and Liza had just pulled in, so the four of us waded through mud to look over my place as the rain poured down. I was anxious to get my screenhouse up so I could permanently move my food and cooking aromas far from my tent. We set up the tent-like contraption quickly, then stood under it and watched the rain. Donna and Liza left, and soon Toni, McKay and I brought our muddy feet into the tent and went to bed.

June 17

Toni and I launched my canoe and about ten pulls later my

decrepit motor gasped and lurched to life, and I gasped and lurched for the steering handle. We cruised upstream a few miles, then shut off the engine and paddled back.

Richard had left a note for me saying it was too wet to work. Begrudgingly, I had to agree.

June 18

Donna stayed overnight, and at 2:30 A.M. a raccoon, or coons, paid the third nocturnal visit in three days. McKay barked, so I tried to shine the flashlight where it had been two nights ago. Donna said, "Closer," so I moved the beam of light in a path towards the tent until it finally came to rest on a big fat coon just in front of the door of the tent, calmly chewing on tidbits of spilled cat food.

After a while it moved over to McKay's doghouse and then it became hard to spot as it climbed up a tree. Donna searched with the light, and suddenly exclaimed, "What's that?" My eyes landed on a small, slinking creature, moving slowly towards the coon's tree. Donna shrieked, "A cat! It's a cat!"

"Chisholm," I echoed. "Oh, no!"

She must have been out since before the coons came, when I had gone to the outhouse. Now my stupid, declawed house cat had treed a coon and was stalking it.

I called my suppertime "Kitty, kitty, kitty" to her and she hesitantly altered her course and came within reach, where I grabbed her and hauled her in.

We had coons at the door for a couple hours, loudly announced by McKay. Finally the chewing outside the door ended, and McKay settled down.

The birds began their morning chorus.

June 19

Donna and I figured out the weight of my logs by putting a four-foot section on her bathroom scale and then multiplying.

The twenty-four-footers are about 910 pounds, and the sixteen-footers are 610. It's nice to know. They're lighter than I thought.

Richard came last night and was angry. He said I had "chewed out" his wife on the phone June 15. I hadn't meant to release any of my negative feelings in her direction, but apparently she correctly read my attitude. I should apologize, but I'll wait until tomorrow after I've had a shower in Duluth. I don't look or smell very forgivable today. I did apologize to Richard, though. That seemed to satisfy him and he proceeded to install my culvert and smooth the gravel.

My hope today is that it won't rain until Mike gets the last loads of gravel out here.

June 20

Mike delivered three loads of gravel, then got a flat tire on his gravel truck. No more gravel. Lots more rain.

The basement is filling up and the sides starting to cave in. I just worked up a sweat digging some trenches in my road so the water can drain off. This is no way to build a house.

What's right? I'm warm. I've eaten. The tent is dry.

June 21

It's not raining, but dark and cold. The old gray stocking cap and down vest are on again. The animals are sleeping. It's almost time for all of us to eat. Something hot tonight.

June 22

Today I encountered a major domestic emergency. My tent zipper broke. This is no laughing matter, with vicious mosquitoes clamoring to get in and senile cats clamoring to get out. I immediately drove to town, where I purchased a heavy-duty army surplus zipper and an awl for sewing it. It took three hours to sew the miserable thing into place, but the emergency is over, and the sky even cleared up during the process.

June 23

There were no more excuses. It wasn't cold; my feet weren't muddy; it wasn't raining. So I went over to apologize to Mrs. Swain for my bad attitude. She dropped her eyes when I brought it up, and I saw that she had felt wronged. When I spoke the words, "Will you forgive me?" her head came up and she smiled and said, "Oh, yes, you don't have to worry about that." The air is now clear between us, and I feel better.

I hope I've learned, too. I can't remember exactly what I said or how I said it to offend Mrs. Swain in the first place, so it wasn't a major incident and I didn't do anything outrageous. The point, for me, is that I allowed my impatience with the weather, with postponements and slow progress to affect my interaction with another person.

If the weather disgusts me and I have to be mad, I must direct my anger towards the weather. To direct it, in whatever small way, towards someone who isn't responsible for the problem is inexcusable.

Afternoon. Eddie Larson came over with a gas-powered pump and pumped all the water out of my basement hole. Now if the weather holds, it'll have a chance to dry out.

We went fishing in the evening and, as usual, the fish weren't interested in my line. I'm glad my survival doesn't depend on the fish I catch. I'd be dead.

June 24

Sunday. 59 degrees. I'm just getting ready for church. First a two-mile run with McKay to work up a sweat. Next, a shampoo and bath in the river. A little lotion. Now I have to think of something to wear on this clean body.

I heard two fun comments at church. When the service ended, the lady next to me introduced me to two young men sitting in front of us. One of them remarked, "I was listening to you sing. You sound just like Tatum O'Neil."

I innocently set myself up for the kill. "Oh, does she sing?"

"No."

As I humbly made my way toward the door two old ladies came up to me and said, "You should come every Sunday. We can tell you've been a church-goer because you sing all the hymns without looking at the words."

They must know all the words too, if they managed to watch me during all the hymns!

June 25

The basement has been drying out nicely, although I still sink up to my ankles in mud in the west end. Mike brought the rest of the gravel in today, and I'm expecting Richard and his Cat any minute. There is great hope for a completed driveway. The basement may be beyond hope. The world is preparing for a heavy rain. It's been blowing hard and dark clouds have rolled in. I was hoping to get the basement finished this Saturday, but with more rain it just can't be.

I caught up on a few letters today — I must write if I want to be written to.

McKay is turning out to be every bit as good a dishwasher as my old Irish Setter, Forbes, was. She has also taken over the responsibility of keeping the cats away from the tent zipper at night.

June 26

The weather is remarkable. Thunder rumbled and lightning flickered half the night, but it never rained, even though heavy rain and hail were predicted. I awoke to a steamy hot, sunny morning. Dry my basement, sun.

The mirror told me I looked presentable, so I put on a dress and drove twenty-five miles to McGregor High School, where I gave my resume to the superintendent. I also spoke to the principal for a few minutes. I wasn't applying for a specific job, but if they know I'm available, it may open a door sometime in the future.

I got home just ahead of Mike Swain, who was coming with the back hoe. He worked on my road a couple hours, then said he was going to lunch. It's now 5:30 P.M. and he's not back. He still needs to dig a drainage trench from my basement. Dave Williams is coming soon to set up footing forms, and the back hoe is sitting in the middle of the driveway. Much as I like Mike, I wish he was a little more zealous about his work.

I reserved a ready-mix truck for Thursday . . . oh, my . . . the back hoe just started. Mike must have returned.

The drainage trench is now in progress.

Humor of the day: my coons found my food cache last night and managed to get the lid off just enough to reach an arm in. They pulled a jar of syrup out of their way. It was sitting neatly beside the food can. Then they had removed and eaten my rye bread, and half a dozen apples (leaving the peelings next to the syrup).

June 27

Mike finished the trench, but wasn't able to get the back hoe up the hill. Now he has to come back after work tonight. I hope he gets it out quickly, because I could use a couple more loads of gravel before the ready-mix truck comes.

I ordered the cement blocks this morning.

Here's the latest schedule:

Tonight: Set up footings.
Thursday: Pour footings (6:00 P.M.)
Friday: Blocks delivered; pick up mixer.
Saturday: Lay blocks.

It's been a lazy day. There's really nothing to do but read and enjoy the pleasant weather, until Dave comes to set up the footing forms.

8:30 P.M. — Major setback number forty-two. Dave said the floor of the basement isn't solid enough for pouring footings. Richard came and dug out two giant piles of gooey muck, and left to get some gravel. He's going to dump two loads in the basement for me to spread out and tramp down. This place is quite a sight. I've got mounds of muck all over in front of my tent, and where Mike got stuck it looks as if someone tossed a half dozen grenades at my hill. This is war.

I've got a crew of friends coming Saturday to lay blocks, but I'll have them do other chores.

June 29

Today I started spreading gravel. Actually, it was more like moving a mountain. I wanted to get the main holes filled before it rained. At 7:00 P.M. it began to pour, but I continued shoveling for an hour. Then I ran out to my truck and carried back a five-gallon bucket of hot water I had brought from Duluth. Standing in the rain in my shorts and shirt, I had a wonderful hot shampoo with a soft rain rinse. A shampoo like that is hard to beat. Thoroughly frozen except for my head, I left my soggy clothes outside and got myself dry and warm in the tent.

Now if I could just call room service for a pizza . . .

June 30

Group tasks:

1. With hammer and chisel, knock the knots off the rafters.
2. Spread gravel in basement.
3. Run fifty laps around circumference of basement to pack gravel.
4. Move poplar poles and roll house logs over.

   5. Screen sand.

A weary day. Lynne came up with Darla, Sharon, Louise and Shirley, and we spread all the gravel in the basement. [Lynne teaches college in Minneapolis and is blessed with an ability to round up willing workers.] Unfortunately, the new surface seems as soggy as the old, only it's soggy gravel instead of soggy clay.

We dug a narrow trench to try and drain the water out. I'm not sure how it's working. But we did all we could, then went for a two-mile jog and an invigorating swim in the river.

It was fun to have a birthday cake after supper, and of all the surprises, my brother Duncan called from San Diego to wish me a happy birthday.

Donna asked me if, at twenty-nine, I had any regrets. At that moment I wish I could have summoned Frank Sinatra to step from a limousine and croon a few bars about having too few regrets to mention.

July 1

I got up at the crack of 8:30 A.M. and jumped into the basement, still in my pajamas, to shovel gravel and open the drainage trench. Then I took a quick dip in the river. Donna and I said goodbye to the Minneapolis group, then worked hard to level a portion of the driveway by hand. I packed it down with the tractor. Dave Williams showed up about 4:30 P.M., just in time to hear me let out an inhuman roar as I slipped into the gooey slime down in the trench. The three of us worked four hours and got the footings formed up. Dave said if it didn't rain the cement could be poured into the wooden forms tomorrow.

July 2

It's raining. Pouring. We got out my roll of plastic and built a huge canopy over the basement. We worked in the rain, trying not to slip in the mud. Everything got slick with mud — the shovels,

Donna in the mud

hammers, boots, our faces. The canopy is effective, so far.

Donna left after we finished, and the sun peeked out for a moment, creating a sauna under the plastic.

July 3

The rain has come in torrents all day. I'm beginning to think I live in the jungle instead of Minnesota and it's the monsoon season. The radio says it will rain tonight and tomorrow, too.

I've had nothing to do but watch my plastic canopy cave in, mud slide into my hole, and brown water rush out the drainage trench. The river is up, and flood warnings are out.

I've just finished reading John Goddard's account of his exploration of the Nile River, and it seems so incredible to read of his struggle with weeks and weeks of intense heat and rainless days in the desert. I could use a few rainless days.

July 4

The rain is so relentless I find myself thinking of it as a person instead of just weather. I get disgusted at the rain and expect it to stop. Doesn't Rain have a choice? Can't Rain go somewhere else? Why does Rain want to prevent me from building my house?

The muddy desolation around here is eroding my basement hole and patience as well. I feel as if I'm in an Italian foxhole, waiting in the mire for more of Mussolini's mortars to rain from the sky. My war is mental, but I'm too wet to fight. I'm going to desert. AWOL.

I'm going to go to Duluth and try to come back with a more positive outlook.

July 5

I got home about noon, and was amazed to see how well things had dried. I spent an hour bailing water out of the basement, but it felt

Building footing forms

solid. Then I shoveled dirt for the rest of the afternoon to fill the floor area between the footings. It wasn't bad shoveling, but occasionally I'd get a shovelful of sticky clay. When I'd swing the shovel to throw the clay down in, it would stick tight to the shovel, almost pulling me off balance and over the side.

It was a hot, sweaty job, but it felt good to be working. McKay and I went for a run, then I jumped in the river and cleaned up.

I reserved the ready-mix truck for tomorrow, in a show of cock-eyed optimism.

July 6

Hallelujah! After shoveling dirt and clay all day, I was rewarded with the ready-mix truck coming and pouring the cement footings.

At last I have some tangible progress. The footings are part of my house. Blocks can be laid on the footings, and logs can be set on the blocks.

I feel such relief to see the building process underway. The slightest progress has a way of making the waiting and the mud and the rain and the mosquitoes all worthwhile.

Making Hay

July 7

Back in April when I used one of the neighboring farmer's brush cutter, I told him I'd help him bale hay sometime. So today I labored in the fields, a grand way to spend a day. I expected to be throwing bales of hay around, but instead, got the easy job of driving the tractor.

Lulled by the vibration and noise of the engine, I could have gone to sleep, but kept awake singing all the songs on my favorite Judy Garland record.

At about 5:30 P.M. I went home and set up the drain tile around my footings and then cleaned the hay out of my hair with a swim in the river. Finally, I sat peacefully in my screenhouse eating soup and preparing the Sunday School lesson for tomorrow.

The peace ended delightfully when six kids appeared en masse from the nearest farm and piled into my screenhouse dining room with me. For the next hour and a half they sat and told me all the funniest things they could think of. Six-year-old Woody didn't get many chances to speak, but once in a while he'd break in with something pertinent, such as: "We didn't get much mail today." Or, "I saw you this morning."

I was thoroughly entertained.

Interaction with kids is something I enjoy. Their conversation is unpretentious and their attitude toward life uncynical. It's one of the reasons I became a teacher nine years ago.

I had many reasons for leaving teaching, one of them being my desire to be doing what I'm doing now. But sometimes I miss the open dialogue with kids that I used to have.

Maybe to the kids around here, I seem like a strange recluse, hidden back in the woods, so they don't come by.

Come to think of it, maybe that's what I am. In any case, "Boo Radley" had a treat today.

July 8

I showed up at church promptly at 9:45 A.M., ready for my class. McKay was in the truck, as I was planning to leave for Duluth right after the service.

I had no sooner sat down than Ann Speedling came over to me and said, "Laurie, do you know your truck is on fire?"

Skillfully maintaining my composure, I replied, "I'll go take a look."

Just as she said, smoke was pouring out from under the hood. As soon as I got the hood open flames leaped up and Mr. Wills tried to beat the fire out with a burlap sack. I grabbed McKay out of the cab, and Mr. Wills ran to get some water.

An eternity later, he returned and splashed the water around the carburetor and extinguished the fire. I envisioned myself getting home by canoe or by foot, but first I went back into the church to teach my lesson. It appropriately dealt with keeping material wealth in its proper perspective.

After church, I picked the burnt hoses and wires out of the engine, and found the charred culprit, a mouse's nest.

July 10

I pried most of the forms away from the footings — no easy task. By 9:00 A.M. it was already a muggy, hot day. Nevertheless, I got out my rake and hoe and attacked the weeds in my garden, then spent the 90-degree afternoon driving tractor for the Soulens. The swim in the river never felt as good as it did this evening. I got cleaned up and visited the Andersons.

July 11

Mother and her friend Bob came for a brief visit. The weather was considerably more pleasant than the last time they came. We took a short cruise up the Mississippi. Mother said my lagoon reminded her of the "African Queen."

Beaching the canoe turned into a bit of slapstick. Bob got out, Mother got out, and then, as I was attempting to turn the canoe around, Bob accidentally gave the bow a light push. The push, with the weight of the motor and me in the stern, was just enough to capsize the canoe. Bottoms up went the canoe, the motor, and me.

Well, it was a hot day.

July 12

I slept late, then installed my drain down in the basement. It was 92 degrees in the shade, so McKay and I took a swim.

In the afternoon I unloaded a couple of hay wagons with the Soulens. Of course, hot, muggy weather usually breaks with rain. My basement is flooding again. If it doesn't stop raining we won't be able to get the blocks laid Saturday.

When I got home from haying, I opened the tent door and there stood McKay. Her leash, with the collar still buckled and clipped to it, was hanging over by the dog house. This is a mystery. If McKay slipped out of the collar, how did she zip the tent? And if someone came and put her inside, why did they remove the collar and leave it buckled?

The cats were indignant about being left out in the rain. They were fairly dry under the poncho, but upset, nevertheless.

The Barretts were visited by a good-sized bear last night. It took

a screen off one of the windows and banged around trying to get in. I suppose it could wander over this way if it comes around again.

Supper in the rain. Creamed corn and dates.

July 13

The sky this morning was as thick and white as mashed potatoes. At about 11:30 A.M., the cloud cover broke apart, letting the sun peek through. With that, my homesite seemed like a tropical rain forest, almost steaming as the sun's rays touched the wet foliage and humid air.

I was steaming, too, hauling buckets of water up the hill to fill a fifty-five-gallon drum. I slipped occasionally, but managed to stay on my feet.

I was very impressed by a spider's web I observed while doing this chore. A web had been spun across the top of the drum, but as I poured bucket after bucket of water over it, it never broke. Finer than thread, and beautifully designed, it was undisturbed by my deluge.

It's similar in some ways to my dream of building a log cabin. It's a simple, delicate dream, nearly transparent. It has an appearance of being fragile, and over the years could be overlooked as temporal; something I would outgrow and abandon. But I did the spinning of my dream. I see it clearly and know its strength. I know its purpose, and it can't be disturbed by deluges of skepticism, setbacks, difficulties, or even my own doubts.

The tent, living quarters for six months

Building the basement

The Basement

July 14

After twelve hours of labor, my property gave birth to a beautiful basement.

Donna mixed all the mud, Mary and I tended, while Dave and George laid the blocks. Mary's dad and his sister-in-law from Denmark helped for a couple hours. It was quite a varied group. Emil told me my drain tile was upside down, so he went around and set it properly. We got all the water we needed at the Larsons. Everything I had hauled up from the river had leaked out overnight. Wonderful.

The job got very hard once the guys were on the scaffold. We had to lift the blocks up to shoulder height, but the end was always in sight so the work was bearable.

I took Mary and Donna out for dinner after everything was done. They had more than earned it. I can feel the muscles stiffening up, but I think perhaps the most grueling job is over. It's hard to believe the basement is actually completed, three months after I moved.

Now I can build my log cabin!

July 15

It took me an hour of thought before I could summon the willpower to lift my body out of bed. Rigor mortis had set in overnight, but the stiffness didn't last long. The Thompsons called and invited me to dinner, so I went to the river and scrubbed the cement off my arms. After a great meal of fresh Northern Pike, I excused myself and returned home. I got back into my dusty overalls and back-plastered the outside of the foundation. I finished about 7:00 P.M., and then took it easy. It suddenly occurred to me that for the first time in quite a while, it was cool enough for a jacket.

July 16

I think I was stiffer today than yesterday, but I got up early and headed for town to return the cement mixer. Before going home, I stopped at Lampert's lumber yard to buy styrofoam to insulate the block walls. Another woman was there getting the same thing. She told the men who were tying down her load, "I wish my husband wouldn't send me on these errands, I'm afraid to back the truck up." Then she said to me, "Are you building too?" I nodded. She shook her head and said, "Why do our husbands make us do all this?"

I just smiled and she chatted on with the men as I drove away.

At home, Donna came and we began to work on the floor. First all the joists had to be cut to length. Then we coated the ends with penta [a wood preservative] and set them into place. We laid planks over a third of the floor space, getting the feel of it, looking out the "windows," opening the "door," and so forth.

We had used the gin pole earlier to hoist twenty-six leftover blocks out of the basement, so I stacked them in a pile out of the way. They should be the last blocks I'll move for a while.

July 17

I worked all day, and felt good doing it. First I finished up the subfloor and got it covered with plastic, then I coated the foundation with tar. I was a mess. A swim in the river felt awfully good.

After supper I visited the Herders to see when Don could slab my logs. Don said he'd have to cut some of the twenty-four-footers in half if the logs had any bow. He said he'd come over in the morning and check for straightness with a string.

July 18

Today Don Herder split my long plate log in half and slabbed the two end logs.

[*Notches are cut half way into each log, so two half-logs must be used opposite each other on the first course. This gets the notching started properly, and provides a flat sill on top of the cement blocks. I used half-logs on the long sides of the cabin. A thin slab was sawed off each of the shorter end logs, so there would be a tight, flat fit against the blocks on the ends, too.*]

He did all the cutting he's going to do for me, because he can't slab all the logs without cutting them in half. My mind is set on building with whole logs and cutting the windows out later, so that's that. I've gone full circle in my decision of fitting the logs.

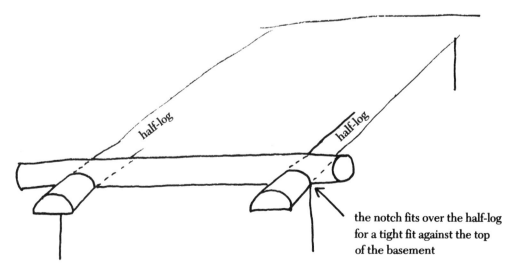

the notch fits over the half-log for a tight fit against the top of the basement

First, I assumed I'd be chinking. Then I read about chinkless construction and decided to cut grooves lengthwise in all my logs. Next, Don said he could slab them so they would be flat on the top and bottom. It sounded very practical. Now I'm back to round logs and chinking. It will be easier, faster, with more wall height, and actually truer to the most traditional rustic workmanship. The fewer machines and sophisticated techniques, the better. I want a primitive cabin — rough, crude and built with my own hands rather than with giant, diesel-powered conveniences.

It's a question of hard versus easy, and a question of pride.

There are easier ways to build a log cabin than the way I have chosen. I could rent a tractor with a loader to lift my logs or ask Don to bring in his log loader. For that matter, I could have ordered a pre-cut, pre-notched log home kit. I could have hired a construction crew. All those options would make it easier to complete my cabin.

I could enjoy living in an "easier" log cabin, but I would never experience the rewards that follow a difficult struggle. I want to struggle. I want that to be a part of my home. The choice is whether to "buy" a home, or "build" a home.

July 19

I have to laugh at myself. Yesterday I was full of bravado about the rewards of a difficult struggle. Today, with the rain streaming through my hair and soaking my jacket, I let Don use his crane to move two logs.

He had come over with the log he split lengthwise yesterday, and together we set the two halves in place. Then he had said, "As long as I'm here, shall I set two end logs into position for you?"

The crane was right behind him. It was pouring rain. It was so easy to say, "Yes."

I think I've just learned the principle of expediency.

July 24

The past four days have been a cultural shock. I traveled from Duluth to Minneapolis, to Rochester, and finally home.

Mother had invited me to go to "Chorus Line" with her at the Orpheum Theater in Minneapolis. So, from my quiet life I found myself threading through Aquatennial traffic [the Aquatennial Parade is *THE* event of the summer in Minneapolis] and seeing a show about the trials and joys of New York chorus line dancers.

Now I'm back to my own trials and joys. My tractor won't start and the chainsaw is in the repair shop. Trials.

Mandy Andrews brought me some raspberries, and I picked four pea pods from my garden. Joys.

Logs at Last

July 25

This has been a quiet, satisfying day. I was rousted early, as I heard John Andrews beaching his canoe down below my tent. He had recharged my tractor battery so it started with a healthy roar. Before having breakfast, I weeded my garden and found one more pea pod worth eating. Finally, I attacked my two freshly scribed notches. As I finished the two notches, Bill Thompson dropped by for his daily inspection.

Now I'm taking it easy, listening to Shostakovich while I wait for President Carter's news conference. A little Mogen David should help me get through it.

July 26

Donna came out and we concentrated on fitting the first end log into place. We struggled getting the notches to fit, because we kept having to lift the log on and off the anchor bolts. In the midst of our problems, it started to rain steadily, and I found myself sliding all over in the wet clay. My marking crayon became useless on the wet logs. At one point when we were trying to raise the log off the bolts, two cement blocks came loose. That upset me. The mortar would have to be chiseled out and replaced. The rain became a real detriment to thought and action, so we quit.

It was my decision to quit, not Donna's. The rain seems to rob me of my concentration, and a calamity like knocking blocks loose defeats me. I question my ability and lose confidence in myself.

When I come to these mental barriers, Donna steps back and waits. She patiently endures while I mutter to myself, or yell, or throw clay at the sky. If I have to quit for the day, she agrees, and if I choose to keep working, she's right there. But she never interferes with my outbursts.

July 27

It has been a wild, wild day. I don't know whether to be elated or sick about it. First, Donna and I made the final adjustments on yesterday's end log, and bolted it into place. Things went much better with the second end log after three tries. The anchor bolts were a nuisance, but we now knew how to deal with them.

The time had finally come to try the gin pole [boom]. We dragged a twenty-four-foot log to the loading area and decided to try a test pull with the tractor before loading up the winch. As I put the tractor in first gear, and moved slowly away from the log, the strain seemed to fill the air. The poles tensed and bowed slightly, the cables stretched taut, and the base tree bent over incredibly. Finally, as the log left the ground, we heard a loud crack. Nothing happened. I put the tractor in reverse and lowered the log to the ground. We found a ten-foot crack up the side of the tree. We retired the gin pole.

Undaunted, we cut two long elm logs to use as ramps, and set up a pulley system. We anchored ropes to the ends of the log we had just notched into place. Onto those ropes went the pulley. The rope through the pulley was tied to the twenty-four-foot log at one end and the tractor at the other.

I inched forward with the tractor and the log crept up the ramps. With much adjusting, pushing, pulling, and heaving, we got it into a position where it finally rolled onto the building.

We found one horrible problem. The top course of blocks, to

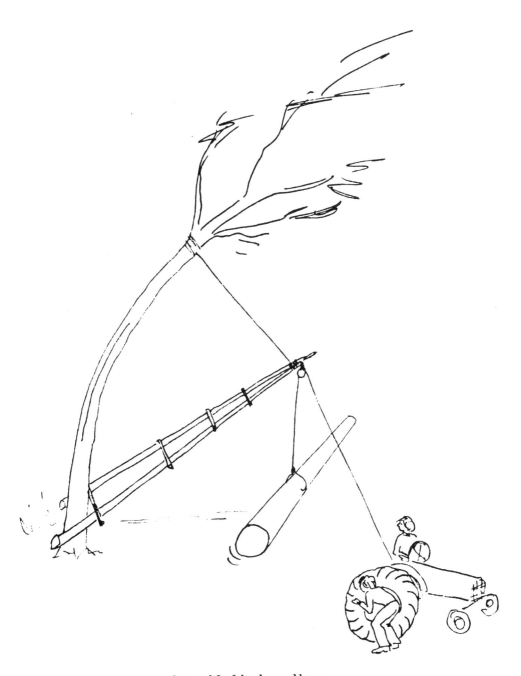

The test lift of the doomed boom

which everything was anchored, had come loose. Eight loose blocks. Tilted. Cracked. Yuk.

The blocks all will have to be remortared and some may have to be replaced. Structurally, the basement is fine, since only the top course is affected, but it's hard for me to be nonchalant about the damage. I feel depressed when I look at it.

The mosquitoes formed up for the 8:30 attack.

Donna and I had a can of spaghetti.

July 30

After a weekend in Minneapolis, I came home for a fresh start. I cut down the tree that supported the gin pole and peeled two poles for my new system: shears. Then I went to Cole's hardware for insulation and various other items.

July 31

Donna arrived at 10:30 A.M. and we accomplished a lot. First, we constructed a shears, my second system for lifting up logs. We followed the FM5-34 [the army's engineer field data manual] for a model.

I changed the design only slightly, replacing the forward guy line with a rigid pole attached in back of the shears.

With that objective accomplished, Donna said we should put another twenty-four-foot log on the building.

This we did, using only the come-a-long, and a shove with the back of the tractor. It took two tries. The first put the butt of the log through the basement window. The glass shattered into the basement. I began whistling an old Gershwin tune. The second thrust put the log nicely on top. We adjusted it, and called it a day.

Donna was totally undisturbed by the fact that we had rammed a log through the window. In this instance, I didn't let it faze me either.

August 1

Last night I sat in the tent and stared at the two twenty-four-foot logs in place over the sill logs. I stared a long time. Something looked wrong. I pulled out my books and looked at pictures of log cabins. I identified the problem. I had a butt over a butt, and a tip over a tip.

Wrong.

[*The large (butt) and small (tip) ends of the logs must be alternated at each corner to prevent having a lopsided building. The principle is easily illustrated by building a small model cabin out of wooden matches.*]

Donna came over this morning and together we easily lifted one log over the other and solved the butt-tip'problem. I scribed the notches on the two logs and sliced the scribed area with the chainsaw. Then I shaped them with the hatchet. Donna cupped and smoothed them with a mallet and gouge.

After Donna left I finished the notches by myself and rolled the first log over. I marked the high spots and shaved them down. I rolled the log back and forth about four times before deciding I'd had enough.

I went for a short swim to bring my body temperature down to normal.

My garden is a wreck. One of the neighbor's cows was loose and she ate the tops of my beets and spinach, stepped on my bush peas and urinated on my beans. I suppose to make it up to me, she left a few pies.

My muscles aren't as sore today as they have been, but I feel really tired. My hands seem disjointed. Time for a nectarine, then bed.

August 2

I slept late, until the sun heated the tent past comfort. I finished off the four notches Donna and I started yesterday. It didn't take more than an hour. I cut and set in the fiberglass insulation, then rolled the two logs into their final resting place. Done! There was nothing else I could do without help, so I ran, swam, and read old *Time* magazines.

Now thunder is rumbling and hard rains are seconds away. It's a beautiful sound.

The winds started blowing so fiercely I was afraid a tree might crash through the tent. I took McKay into the basement, but after sixty seconds in that dripping, flooded cave, I decided it would be better to die in the tent.

Anyway, the wind is down now, and it's just raining heavily.

August 3

What did I accomplish today? Nothing. Well, I monkeyed a little with my first layer of chinking and hauled the next two logs back with the tractor, but that's it. I finished off a package of cookies, read a few June *Newsweeks* for the third time, and got real mad at the zipper on the screenhouse. It's just as well there weren't any notches to work on . . . it's been one of those gray, mosquito-infested days.

August 4

There really is strength in numbers. Toni, Connie, Donna and Liza all came to work, and we all did with ease what Donna and I struggle with long and hard.

Liza, Donna and I lifted two end logs up, and when Connie and Toni came, we mass-produced four beautiful notches. In two hours we had fitted the two end logs in place. Then we picked up two long logs and shoved them into position. It was so easy I could hardly believe it.

Of course, I enjoyed seeing such fast progress, but the high point of the day was to see the enthusiasm of my helpers, ex-

Friends help

periencing something so new. Connie, in particular, seemed to relish every moment, from learning how to use a chisel, to swimming in the river at the end of the day.

I shared not just work, but a way of living, and it's a very special feeling to share that.

August 5

My first duty was to take Toni and Connie to the bus stop. I was sorry to see them go — visits are always too short.

I returned home and got right to work. When the mosquitoes insisted I quit, I had one twenty-four-foot log notched securely, and another one roughed out. I'm really pleased with the way the logs are fitting.

Eddie wanted me to see his new husky, so I walked over after supper. When I got home, *my* husky had strewn things all over the tent. I guess I won't leave her alone inside again.

The moon is almost full — what a sight! Can't wait for tomorrow.

August 6

Three courses up; five to go. Now it's getting awkward to go over the walls and onto the floor. Donna slipped as we were pulling a log up, and went sprawling. After that, I built a trap door for the entrance to the basement, so no one ends up falling into the hole.

The weather has been peculiar today. First, it was cold enough for a jacket, then it got so hot I went swimming, and now there are tornado warnings being issued.

August 8

Today I went to town for some hardware and, when I got back, chinked the logs that are in place. I'm using lath over the fiber-

Smoothing the notch

glass temporarily, while the logs go through their shrinking process. In a year I'll do something more permanent.

Mike is busy backfilling again. Soon there will be peace back here. No more piles of dirt, loud engines, or bruised trees.

I cringe when the back hoe scrapes or bangs into trees. I accepted the sacrifice of trees that are in the way of my driveway and cabin site, but when that big yellow machine scrapes the bark off a healthy young oak, I can almost hear it cry out in pain.

I tend the wounds with thick tar, and wish for the back hoe to be gone.

August 10

I was enthralled by the sight of my cabin as I walked around the last bend in the driveway. Now that the area is smoothed and slopes gradually down to the river, it has regained its picturesque charm — solitary wooded peninsula, overlooking the Mississippi. Another treat waiting for me tonight was a full supper ready in the garden.

August 11

This has been a day of preparation for stage two of the wall effort. It's no longer possible to shove the logs up manually. Donna and I will try the shears tomorrow. To get ready, I chained a large basswood log horizontally behind the tractor and dragged my driveway and new yard. Then I spread some grass seed around. Finally, I dragged the next three wall logs into position to be lifted.

My garden gave me potatoes, beans and carrots for supper. There's a crispness in the air that reminds me of autumn.

The shears

August 12

The progress is inspiring. All day Sunday Donna and I worked in the rain, setting up the shears. It helped us lift two twenty-four-footers easily. The only effort on my part was to pump the hoist lever, and Donna guided the log with a rope from inside the cabin. It was literally no sweat.

Now that the cabin is officially half done, I'm thoroughly relieved that the shears has worked so well, and I can feel confident about getting the rest of the logs up. It's a victory. Victory over what? Victory over the weight of the logs, a dependence on machines and men (nothing against either one—I just like the challenge of doing this without them). And victory over skeptics who doubted this house would ever happen.

It's happening.

August 14

The day began normally enough. Donna and I got two logs notched in, and two more hoisted up with the shears, making a total of six logs it had lifted. Then I reached the conclusion that the shears were going to be too short to load the higher logs, and we'd have to build a larger device.

I dragged two peeled, twenty-foot logs back to the cabin and the mission impossible began. One at a time we lifted the small end of each log until it rested on the top log of the wall. Next, gripping the larger bottom ends of the two logs with tongs, we pulled and yanked until both logs were leaning against the wall, touching near their balance point, much like a teeter-totter. Donna climbed to the two tops and neatly lashed them together. We looped a long climbing rope over the top of our new shears and tied the other end of that rope around a clump of basswood trees on the far side of the cabin.

Then we pushed, and shoved, and suffered, until the two logs were leaning against the cabin as steeply as we could get them. I staked the bottoms of both logs so they could not slip. We set up another rope that went around the top of the shears, through a pulley fifty feet away and over to the tractor.

Finally, I dug a hole, twelve inches deep, just in front of the lower end of each log. The holes would help anchor the shears.

The concept was that as I drove the tractor away from the cabin, the shears would slowly rise to a nearly vertical position. The concept was tremendous, but the actual lift of our twenty-foot, fifteen hundred-pound shears was far more dramatic.

As I drove the tractor down the driveway, nothing happened. I drove farther and farther away, and the climbing rope stretched like a rubber band, but the shears didn't move. Donna envisioned the pulley breaking loose and whizzing through her body. I pictured snapped ropes severing one of our heads. The rope just kept on stretching.

Suddenly we both screamed in horror as the shears virtually flew upright. The rope from the basswood clump miraculously held and prevented the logs from sailing right on over. Donna and I could only stare. We had launched the shears, and there it stood, positioned exactly the way we wanted it.

After we recovered, we jockeyed the logs into their respective anchor holes, and I climbed cautiously to the top to fasten the pulley and cable.

As the cool night air encircled my little knoll, we had everything anchored in place and ready for a lift.

August 15

Things went slowly today. We did get two more logs notched in, but they both had bows in them and it was tricky getting them to fit down along their lengths.

[*When notches are accurately marked with a scribe, the log should fit down snugly against the log below. A bow or a bulge, or a knot, however, can hang down and prevent the notched*

Hewing

corners from settling down into place. The offending obstacle must be removed by hewing. With an ax or hatchet, several slashes are first cut at an angle into the bulge, one or two inches apart. Then, holding the ax parallel to the log, the bulge can be sliced away until it is flush with the rest of the log. I found this to be very time-consuming, and often flattened one bulge only to find another that I hadn't noticed earlier.]

Donna stayed long enough to put up two more logs with our magnificent new shears, but then had to get back to Duluth.

August 16

I was awakened early by the sound of a large truck rumbling down my driveway. I jumped into some clothes, and ran out and greeted the well drillers.

They worked all day and didn't hit water. While they drilled, I put lath over the fiberglass insulation between the most recent courses of logs, and roughed out four notches.

It has been drizzling and cold most of the day. Now, at 8:30 P.M., it's raining, and I have to wear two wool shirts and a down vest to be warm, but Wagner and Strauss are entertaining me for the evening.

August 18

Donna came today. She's on vacation and won't have to rush back to Duluth right away. We got two logs fitted in, but it was slow going. The first one took a lot of hewing — almost the full length.

At 7:45 P.M. we got a new log winched up on top, but we stopped at that point. I was famished.

During the night I went out to use the outhouse, and on the way back spotted two glowing blue dots, each no bigger than the period a typewriter makes. I fetched the flashlight to investigate, and focused the beam on a quarter-inch brown worm of some sort. Very ugly.

I suppose the lesson to be learned is never to be mesmerized by beautiful eyes in the moonlight.

August 19

Donna and I got to work about 1:00 P.M. The notching went extra fast. We had a good system, moving from notch to notch until they were all done.

[*The notching process can be broken into four steps. First, the area to be notched must be marked with a scribe, or large compass. The points of the scribe are set at the distance between the log to be notched and the log below it. I often set the scribe a quarter- to a half-inch less to avoid a lot of hewing. With a crayon fastened to the top point of the scribe, the lower point is moved carefully along the surface of the log that lies perpendicular to the one being notched. The crayon will make a line on the log to be notched. This must be done from both sides of the log. When the log is rolled over, there should be a rough*

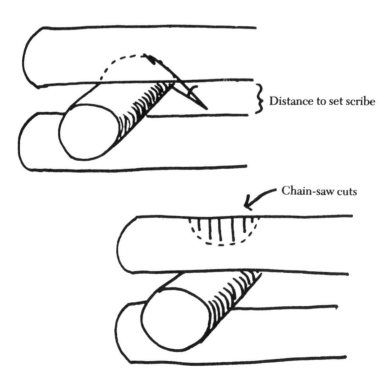

Distance to set scribe

Chain-saw cuts

oval drawn on the log. When properly cut, the notch will fit the precise contours of the log below.

My second step, used only to save time, was to cut into the oval area about four times with a chain saw.

Third, a wedge or heavy hammer is used to knock out the large chunks between the chain saw cuts.

Finally, a hatchet or wide chisel is used to carefully shave the notch down to the outline that was scribed. The center should be slightly cupped, and smooth.]

We had a near calamity putting the second log up. We hoisted it up in a hurry, only to find that it was on backwards, and we would need to turn it around. In the process of shouldering it around, we accidentally jarred the log across from it, and it sat teetering one-quarter inch from the edge of the house.

This building creates one challenge after another, and occasional near calamities. But everything remains under control. Close to the edge, but under control.

Once the logs were notched, I had to leave for a township meeting. Donna worked for two hours by herself. When I returned, under a dark sky, she was just climbing down from the chin-high cabin. She tells me we're going to put the ridgepole up this week.

A loon is laughing in the distance.

August 20

We set a new record today, but it was an old goal. One full course of logs. It wasn't that hard, just a matter of having the whole day to work together, and a minimum of interruptions. Actually the last four notches only took an hour. The most time-consuming jobs are raising the logs into place without either of us getting killed (safety is always time-consuming — a price I can afford) and fitting the entire lengths of the logs so the notches are able to rest down tight without untrimmed knots or bulges hanging the log up between the two notches.

We quit working at dark and ate a big supper without ever seeing what any of it looked like.

My exhausted body is about to melt into a sleeping bag.

August 23

The rain shut down operations for a while. It misted all day today, but we finished the seventh course. I decided we have to go a course higher than I originally planned, so we've got eight more logs to go on the walls.

This was visitors' day, I think. Liza, Jean and Michelle all stopped by.

August 24

Donna and I worked a twelve-hour day, nine to nine. By the time we quit the stars were out, and all I could see of the notch I was cutting was that it was lighter than the rest of the log.

My friend Jim Driver came all the way from Fargo, N.D., and I had the good fortune to be taken out to dinner.

August 25

Donna and I set a new record, starting work at 7:00 A.M. Then we put in an exciting, four-log day.

I shocked Donna and Jim while we were pulling the first log across the building. Just as I pulled the end of the log up to its resting place, my tongs slipped, and I fell nine feet to the ground.

Fortunately, I had had the presence of mind to push away from the building and pretend I was jumping backwards off a diving board. However, there was no water, so I flexed my knees and performed a moderately graceful landing.

For the rest of the day, as I trotted from corner to corner, chain saw in hand, I noticed I had lost just a fraction of my Nadia Comaneci amplitude.

Even so, our accomplishments were very satisfying. We finished the walls.

With only the roof and finishing work left to go, I decided to take a break, and I am heading for the Boundary Waters Canoe Area with a small group of friends.

Canoeing

Going to the BWCA was a wonderful idea. I had time to just sit and look.

Monday morning I lay on a rock and watched a seagull glide on spiraling air currents. Later I saw a bald eagle and two hawks. Early this morning a black bear came up to the tent, and touched the fabric with his paw. Lynne jumped up in time to see him run off, but I was still too groggy to move. I wonder if the bear was a descendant of the mother and cubs who demolished our food pack nineteen years ago when Father, Jamie and I were camped at the same spot. That trip years ago was my introduction to the Boundary Waters Canoe Area. I love traveling different routes, but no matter how often I return to that one place, it's as special as it was the first time I saw it.

I love shivering under the waterfalls in the summer and basking on warm boulders overlooking the Canadian bluffs in the fall. And in the winter I marvel at the magic that three feet of snow bring to the place, while I struggle at the same time with the basics of winter survival.

Here at the cabin, winter still seems remote, even though I'm shivering just slightly as I write.

It took Donna and me a little less than a month to complete the walls. Now, refreshed from my short canoe trip, I'm eager to get going on the roof. The stiffness and swelling of my hands has vanished with four days' rest, my thoughts are fresh and clean, and I feel ready for the next challenge.

Cutting out the doorway

The Next Challenge

August 30

All the problems are challenging. Compared to putting up thirty-six thousand pounds of logs, cutting out a door seems trivial, but even so, it taxed me thoroughly. I think the trouble with it was that I had to stand in such awkward positions while I was running the chain saw. The whole thing was simply awkward. I'm trying to build door and window frames in such a way that the logs can shrink without shifting out of position or binding the doors and windows, but it's . . . awkward. Clumsy. Frustrating.

[*With door frames, you have to prevent the logs from shifting out of alignment, or binding the door as the logs shrink and settle. This can be a problem.*

I cut into the ends of the logs in a straight line from the top of the door to the floor. Then, facing the door, I cut into the logs perpendicularly to the first cut, until the four-by-four-inch chunk fell out of each log. I did this from both sides of the door, so that I had a vertical "tongue" in the ends of the logs. Against both sides of this tongue, I placed a four-by-four. Using the nose of the chain saw, I cut three slots that went through the inside four-by-four, the log tongue, and the outside four-by-four. Into the bottom of these slots went ten-inch bolts. The slots will allow the logs to settle without binding on the bolts.]

I'm near the end of my tolerance with my chain saw. After I went through the ritual of trying to start it without success, I seriously considered taking it back where I got it, hurling it against the wall, and telling some frightened receptionist to keep it.

Bill came along during the afternoon, and soon he and Donna and I were bumping heads trying to peer into one tiny hole. We needed to reconnect the throttle, and Donna finally got the wire through the right spot.

If it weren't for Donna's brother's old Homelight, we'd probably be on the fourth course of logs, chopping every notch out completely with hatchets.

I'll never buy another yellow chain saw. Lemons are yellow.

Well, the lemon is working now, and tomorrow is a new beginning.

It's grand to have a front door.

August 31

All the hard stuff on the stupid door is done. Donna and I had it finished at about 2:00 P.M. It's really a one-person job, but Donna kept the chain saws sharpened and full of gas and oil, and was ready with tools as I needed them. She also kept a ready supply of moral support on hand.

Of course, the door isn't really done. I still need to tighten the bolts, build a frame out of two-by-eights, and then there's the door itself. What I have now is just a sturdy opening.

We spent the afternoon putting in two tie logs, one to support the loft, and one to look nice over the living room.

[*Tie logs are notched and spiked in place across the top of the two long walls. They prevent the walls from spreading outward under the weight of the roof.*]

The latter tie log almost looked nice in the basement. When I cut one end to the proper length, the other end slipped off the wall and crashed to the floor. It was a trick getting it back up in its shortened condition, but we made it easier using the shears and winch, and neither of us died.

It shook me up a bit to think of what might have happened. The

Chain-saw maintenance

log could have broken through the floor, or Donna might have been underneath it when it slipped. Are we very alert and conscientious, or just very lucky?

I hope it's the former, but it's probably the latter.

Donna's vacation is over as of today, so I'll be doing a lot more from now on. Fortunately, most of the heavy lifting is done.

When there's work I can't manage by myself, Donna will make a special trip to be helpful. She's already promised to come on Wednesday.

September 1

I had planned on getting everything set up for the ridgepole raising so when Donna came Wednesday we wouldn't waste time on things I could do alone. But alas, I spent most of the day worrying about a driving rainstorm that threatened to demolish my tent.

The weather broke for a couple hours in the afternoon, and I dragged the ridgepole, my totem pole and a dozen ten-foot logs to the cabin. Those were the last of the logs that had been out by the road. With that done, I will try to sell my tractor. I've become very fond of it, but I have no real use for it any more, and I'm running precariously low on funds.

September 4

Following a hectic weekend at the State Fair, I had what I think is one of the most enjoyable days I've spent here. There have been more exciting days, funnier days, busier days — but today was, in an unspectacular way, grand.

At 10:00 A.M. I had a job interview at McGregor High School. There is a possibility they might hire me as a Title I reading tutor two days a week. That would be ideal, but it isn't definite. I am on the substitute list, however, so if a few teachers get sick now and then, I just may be able to earn enough to eat this winter.

Once I got home, I started getting company, and wondered if I'd get any work done.

Bill came by and told me he didn't think I should cut big openings in my walls. "A waste of the logs," he said. There may be an element of waste, but I'm not about to waste a good view, either. "Please let me do it my way, Bill."

Roger came next and was very enthusiastic about the progress I've made.

"Thanks, Roger, you made my day."

I have to keep my objectivity about these opinions. Everyone has a comment to make.

"Why'd you do this?"

"Why don't you do that?"

"How come you did it this way?"

"Should that be there?"

"What's this for?" "That's nice." "This is strange." "Did you mean to do that?" And on and on and on.

At first, the comments affected me, and I took them to heart. If someone came along and liked something, I figured I had done it right. If something was criticized, I thought I must have done it wrong.

I'm learning to tune out the remarks. Right or wrong is relative. The home I ultimately end up with will reflect a long series of personal choices and decisions. Relative to me, it will be right.

After Bill left, William Keiser, a retired bachelor, stopped by for the first time. He harvests wild rice every fall with Bill. This year Bill can't go, so I asked William if he'd let me be his ricing partner. He rambled on for a moment about people in town "talking," and the sore muscles that go along with ricing, but he was actually rather tickled, if I read his face correctly. I'm to meet him Thursday morning.

He was the last of my company. The work I completed in the afternoon and evening was thoroughly satisfying. It wasn't difficult or frustrating, but required thought, patience and a variety of tools. First, I set up all the pieces Donna and I will need tomorrow to raise the ridgepole. Then I spiked in the joists for my

loft floor. It doesn't sound like a lot of work, but there were many
little things involved, and I didn't finish until dark. What felt so
good was finishing what I started out to do without running into all
kinds of problems and delays.

Now the full moon is shining away, and there's a beautiful,
warm breeze.

September 5

The ridgepole was supposed to be easy. It was hard. Donna came
at 10:00 A.M. and we prepared our support system, then raised
up the log with the shears. We boosted one end of the pole up, but
realized with despair that the shears was too short to get the other
end high enough. So we attempted the impossible. It's always
better to try something impossible than to give up.

Donna and I stood out on a single porch support, nine feet
above the ground, and prepared to lift the low end of the ridgepole up overhead. A mist began to fall. We tried three times to
raise the ridgepole, and each time had to lower it back down. We
had to lift it up. On the fourth try, like Olympic weightlifters
hoisting five hundred pounds between us, we curled the log to our
shoulders, did a snatch to put it under our chins, then did a
military press, forcing the log onto the beam it was to rest on. Our
form wasn't quite up to Olympic standards. At one point the pole
rested on Donna's head. We were both on our tiptoes, and we
both crunched a few fingers.

We got it up. The toughest muscle-move we've made. A mira-
cle. It was four hours from the time we began working. Donna
wept with relief.

As the ridgepole was spiked and anchored into place, it began to
get dark, but we decided to try and put up my totem pole before
we would call it a day.

[*I carved the totem pole several years ago, while living in
Wabasha. Each figure on the fifteen-foot log represents a previous canoe trip to the Boundary Waters Canoe Area.*]

I've had the totem up twice before at my previous homes. In Wabasha, four men came from the Army Reserve unit and pushed it up. It looked like Ira Hayes and his platoon raising the flag on Iwo Jima. Another time Donna and I pulled it up using a rope and her car for the power.

This time there was no Army and no car.

We lifted it up, inch by inch.

Traditionally, the day the ridgepole is spiked into place is a day of celebration, so we went to Quadna, and I spent twenty-two dollars for our dinner.

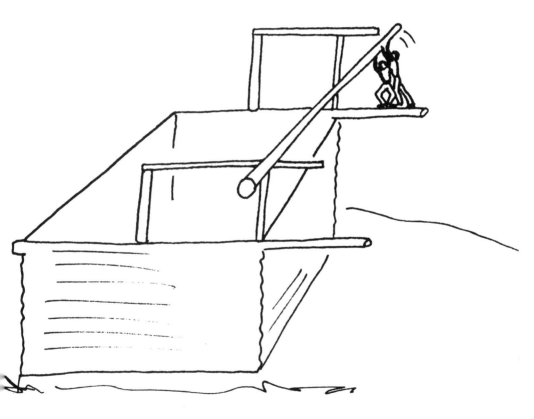

Raising the ridgepole

The walls are finished

Ricing

September 6

My bones creaked and groaned when I pried them out of bed early to meet William Keiser and go ricing.

Every muscle ached from wrestling with the ridgepole, but soon we were out in a large rice paddy, and tired as I was, the scene was soothing in the same way music can be. I poled, observing the rhythm of William's sticks, and listening to the "chut, chut" of the pounding and rattle of the rice raining into the canoe.

In the distance a few other canoes were also ricing in our paddy, but all I could see across the tall rice were the poles moving smoothly up and down. It was like the bows in a string quartet rising in unison, but in this case, the music was of birds, canoes rustling through the swamp vegetation, and sticks beating the wild rice crop.

By the end of the day, my arms were almost numb from six hours of poling, and I was glad to load the canoe and bags of rice on the truck and head for home. Donna was waiting for me and we lifted the last log — a porch rafter support.

The shears can now join my tractor in retirement.

September 7

Today William poled and I pounded. It was easier physically, but my view was reduced to rice, ladybugs, blonde spiders and little black worms. We gathered in seventy pounds, for a pretty good day.

When I got home, I put up half my rafters, but had to quit when it got dark. It seems I have to quit earlier and earlier because of that.

It's going to be another cold night, close to freezing.

September 8

The ricing wasn't too good today. We only harvested about fifty pounds.

I've decided to use eave logs on my cabin to support the base of the rafters, so I rode the tractor across my neighbor's fields. Then I dropped two balsams and had them almost limbed when the chain saw quit on me. The chain jammed or something. With the tractor, I dragged the logs to the cabin. It was too dark to do anything else more, so I had some soup.

September 9

It's illegal to harvest rice on Sunday; so I used the day to make some progress on the cabin.

Donna and Liza drove out, and with three of us working, lifting the eave logs into place was no problem. We bolted them in, Liza left, and Donna and I spiked in the rest of the rafters. Then we headed for Bridgeman's, twenty-five miles away.

[*Bridgeman's is an ice cream parlor and restaurant chain in the Midwest.*]

I disappeared into the ladies' room with a washcloth, and I scrubbed. Then I washed my hair in the sink and realized as I was rubbing it dry that I didn't have a comb with me. I returned to our booth with my hair wet and standing out in every direction, but it felt good to be clean.

Dragging logs

September 10

William and I riced all day. It was cold and windy, but we stayed
with it because the crop is nearly finished and William said it was
really our last chance. Altogether we collected about two hundred
pounds of green rice. That isn't very good, but I enjoyed every
minute of it. I'll miss sitting in the canoe with William, visiting
over our peanut butter sandwiches.

The time passed quickly with his stories of the Depression, the
war, ranching, and farming. The sensitivity in his eyes, the pure
white hair piled under his cap, and the blue trails that meandered
across the backs of his hands often told more than his words, and it
was good for me to listen.

September 11

It drizzled all day today, so I couldn't work on the roof. This cold,
wet weather could give me a case of melancholia, but a letter on
my desk has provided a warm touch to my day.

It's from Connie, who came to help one weekend, and just
seeing her name at the bottom of the short page reminded me of
those few hot, wonderful days when friends and friends of friends
would occasionally come by to work, swim and laugh.

She says: " . . . Sure had a memorable weekend up there with
you. Thanks again for letting me be part of it all."

I love being alone, living alone, and working alone. It makes life
very special. God is always close because there is no one closer,
friends are never taken for granted, and an off-the-cuff sentence at
the end of a letter can be a treasure.

Friends have been around to help in many ways with my cabin,
and I think I'll always love it more for having shared it with them.

September 13

Rain, shine, rain, shine, all day long. It reminded me of the mountains, with their abrupt, unpredictable changes, from rain clouds to sunny skies. It was appropriately disgusting weather to do a disgusting job. I finished the second door opening. It involved the most agonizing cuts with the chainsaw, but even though it was every bit as unpleasant as the first door, I had a feeling of satisfaction when it was completed.

William has changed his mind about the ricing crop and thinks we should give it another try. He wants to go ricing tomorrow, so it appears that I'll experience another cold day on the paddy.

September 14

The rice harvest was pretty light, but it was fun to be out there again. We passed a muskrat house, made of neatly piled swamp grasses, surrounded by a perfect ring of water where the animals had cleared out their materials for the shelter. Beyond the ten-foot-wide "moat" was the wild rice. It reminded me of the early log cabin builders, who picked their building sites in the middle of what seemed to be inexhaustible forests. The trees they felled created isolated clearings in the center of which would go the small dwellings made from the fallen timbers.

If a muskrat house is organized swamp grass, then a log cabin is nothing more than organized trees.

Mine is a little disorganized.

The roof

Roof, Windows, and Autumn

September 15

This is Mother's birthday. It's the first time I've missed it in twenty-nine years. She gave me her blessing to stay home and work on my roof, so that's what I did. Donna and Lynne arrived in the afternoon to help, and together we struggled to get the tongues in the grooves on the roof lumber. We got one side completed before dark, then drove half an hour to a restaurant and stuffed ourselves.

September 16

My help returned and we got to work on the other half of the roof. The third board we used had a nasty warp in it, and ended up throwing the whole side out of level. But, crooked or not, we finished the job, covered it with plastic, and I finally have a roof over my cabin. Now everything can dry out.

For some strange reason, the weather was absolutely perfect today and yesterday — clear skies and mid-seventies.

September 17

Today, working alone, I cut out my picture window and carefully framed it up, so the glass I had would fit perfectly. I made the most stupid mistake imaginable. I was sure the glass height was forty-

five inches, so I didn't put a measuring tape to the glass. The result
was a terrific window frame, three inches too high. The glass is
forty-two inches. Stupid.

I'll fix it tomorrow.

It has been another day of flawless weather. Now that I have a
roof overhead, it probably won't rain for a month.

September 18

It didn't take me too long to fix my window frame. I enlarged the
vent at the bottom to take up the three extra inches. Then I
carefully set in the two large panes of glass, and stepped back to
enjoy the view. Later, I finished my kitchen window frame and
worked a while on the door frame.

The days are getting much too short. I have to quit just when
I'm most engrossed. Along with the short days there is a delightful
shortage of mosquitoes, and a lovely touch of yellow and red in the
leaves.

The river has been getting progressively colder since about the
last week in August. I'm still swimming regularly, though, as a
way of holding onto summer, I suppose.

Tonight, as in previous September nights, I plunged in at
midnight for a brief, paralyzing dip.

I could swim during the warmest part of the day, but I prefer to
let the mercury drop to 45 degrees or so — midnight — and
challenge the cold head-on.

Then, with numb, unfeeling skin, I do a lazy backstroke and
marvel at the number of stars in the sky. They seem to lunge out of
their orbits, as if van Gogh had painted them, and I become aware
of their vastness and beauty during my nocturnal September
swims.

September 19

The windows are all cut out and framed up now. I bought and

The picture window

The gable end

worked on some lumber for the gable ends, and swept all the sawdust up, on the main floor and in the basement.

Then, for a change, I stopped to have supper while it was still light. I chiseled my thresholds smooth after eating, and then, suddenly, it was dark.

I did a little math today, too. Last weekend, I was in the basement and found half a dozen frogs hopping around. Apparently, they either fell in the trap door, or down the space around the sub-floor.

I was thinking about those frogs today, and did a little calculation on the back of a bank deposit slip. I found that if a four-inch-tall frog falls seventy-two inches into my basement, it would be the same as a person falling about ninety-six feet. The person would be killed; the frog goes about his business as usual.

What a remarkable creature.

September 20

I got off to a late and lazy start, sleeping in until 10:00 A.M.

I had to leave at 5:00 P.M. for Duluth, so once I started work I kept hard at it, and still managed to get quite a bit done. First I put the glass in the kitchen window, then I got one whole gable end framed up, and a couple pieces of insulation board nailed in place over the studs.

At one point I pinched my hand, and a large blood blister formed at the base of a finger. I realized the extent of my callouses when I thrust the point of my knife under the skin to drain the blood, and there was no pain at all. I might just as well have stabbed the sole of my boot.

September 21

This afternoon I finished closing in the gable end with insulation board.

Then Donna appeared for a symbolic event. We untied the

safety rope from the shears, and with one hand, I pushed them over. It was like the end of an era to see the contraption fall.

But we didn't grieve. We leveled eight porch support blocks, chiseled and wedged four logs to rest across the blocks, and laid the separated shears logs across the top, creating a massive porch floor structure.

September 22

After going to bed last night I was amazed to hear a car driving down my driveway. I heard it stop by my tent, and then the doors opened and slammed shut. No one ever drives their car in. Finally, a voice said, "Laurie? It's Sue McGraw."

There were Sue and Lori, women who used to be my favorite kids to babysit, ready to look at my cabin in the dark. What a great surprise it was.

Today was a little rainy, but Donna and I notched in all the porch logs. I spiked everything together and we quit work after the rafters were in place.

I hadn't expected to finish the whole thing so fast. The rain made everything slippery and dangerous, Donna has been sick and wasn't feeling very well, and I was impatient with the problems we encountered. Even so, I was really happy with the results of our work.

September 23

I accomplished an assortment of jobs today. While it was still dark, I got up and went to William's house. We had an appointment to get our wild rice processed. He was just about to have breakfast, so he invited me to sit down and have an egg.

He placed an egg on the plate before me. It was fried. Really fried. I tried three times to cut it with a fork, and was grateful that he was busy with his own egg and wasn't watching. I was grateful again to find a knife by my plate, with which I was able to saw the egg into pieces.

William seemed to enjoy his egg, and it occurred to me that anyone joining me for one of my one-pot suppers could very likely regret the experience. I guess we tend to acquire a taste for our own inadequacies.

We soon left and had the rice processed.

September 24

I worked all day on the second gable end, and just short of finishing it I ran out of daylight.

I put in the studs, insulation board and half the boards.

The fall weather was perfect, one of those final warm days before the frost stays past sunrise.

September 25

I closed in the gable end pretty quickly, and then proceeded with a demonstration of my ineptness.

Actually, I'm satisfied with the work I did, and I had a grand, creative time doing it, but I violated the customary expectation that door frames should be plumb and level.

I also violated reasonable standards of cleanliness today . . . this week.

The musty scent that surrounded me reminded me of my days as a school bus driver, in particular of picking up football teams after an early-season practice scrimmage. But I knew I'd take a shower in Duluth tonight, so I tolerated myself.

September 30

The trees have all turned a brilliant gold, and the slightest breeze touches off a shower of falling leaves. I don't think an artist could ever completely capture the beauty of fall on canvas, because so much of its dazzle is motion.

One of the most exciting autumn events is the migration of the birds. I watched a flock of ducks head south in the morning, the platoon sergeants honking out the cadence as the troops maintained a perfect formation.

I was working at 8:00 A.M., building shelves for all my possessions. Then I moved all the boxes down to the basement to their new home.

That done, I made braces for the porch posts. I don't think they serve any functional purpose, but they lend a sturdy, finished touch to the porch.

By mid-afternoon the visitors started coming — nine in all. Michelle and Dawn brought their van loaded with my things and we filled the rest of my storage space.

I've certainly had my share of visitors since moving to this relatively remote area. I'm a novelty. Old friends and new come to see the-girl-who-built-the-log-cabin. Once I've been here a while I expect the visits to taper off. In the meantime it's a novelty to me to have such frequent company. I'll enjoy it while it lasts.

October 1

Two firsts: the first of October, and the first campfire I've built since I moved. Why I waited so long to have fire, I'll never know. I had one tonight because I was cold, and didn't feel like going to bed. I sat and sat and sat and enjoyed the fire immensely. It was so warm. As I listened to the "mony wee beasties aboot," I was blissfully content.

October 2

I spent a few hours in Grand Rapids buying more supplies. When I got home, I nailed sheets of galvanized steel onto the porch

The porch

rafters. Then I tried another heating idea. I lit up a small kerosene heater I got for a dollar at an auction.

The tent warmed to a balmy 65 degrees, but within ten minutes it was so smoky I couldn't see across the tent. That will never do.

October 3

At 5:30 A.M. I was stumbling around, trying to wake up, get dressed and stay warm. Daryl Purvis had asked me to ride his bus route with him so I could be a substitute driver for him occasionally.

When I got to his house, I went in and saw, under the kitchen light, that my skin was a uniform shade of gray from my smoky experiment with the kerosene heater. I'm sure I made a wonderful first impression on Daryl and his wife.

Morning and afternoon bus trips made it hard to get much done. I built the north door and managed to get it hung, but I wasn't real pleased with the one-inch gap at the bottom. There was no time today to solve that problem.

October 5

I struggled and struggled to hang my front door. Eventually, I got it to quit binding, after exhausting my supply of personally acceptable expletives: awrgh, rrrr, ayaahg, and so on. I also closed in the gaps between the north rafters, and insulated one gable end.

The weather during the day was beautiful, but as evening neared, it degenerated into a cold stormy night. The idea of finding something to eat in my dark, wind-chilly screenhouse didn't appeal to me, so I transferred my entire kitchen facility to the cabin basement, lit the kerosene heater, and enjoyed a cozy sub-surface, sub-standard meal.

October 6

I hear it got up to 106 degrees in Arizona today. In northern Minnesota, it's 32 degrees and dropping.

In anticipation of colder temperatures ahead, I did some more insulating in my cabin.

Mary and Janet stopped over unexpectedly and after a tour of the cabin, invited me to Mary's folks' for supper. What a treat it was to spend a few hours in a warm house.

I had an even bigger treat earlier when my well driller came and hooked up the pump. Finally.

It may take a while to get used to having a ready source of water.

October 7

It was a year ago today that I first came and looked at this piece of property. It has changed — but what drew me to it, remains the same.

Today Dave Williams started building the chimney. He built it almost to the ceiling, then fixed the top course of wall blocks that Donna and I had knocked apart so long ago.

In the afternoon Jamie came up to help, so carrying the chimney blocks wasn't an overwhelming task.

The most surprising event of the day was having to chip a quarter of an inch of ice off the top of McKay's water bucket. The temperature dropped to about 20 degrees overnight. I'd better dig up my potatoes.

October 8

The day began terribly. Jamie and I started to lay floor boards, and by noon we had covered about eighteen inches. Nothing fit. Then, by the grace of God, everything started to work. The boards fit nicely, and we got around the trap door and the chimney with no trouble. The only thing that was unpleasant was a bitter north wind. We were within six feet of finishing, but it became so dark we couldn't see the nails.

October 9

What a wasted day! On the way to town to get more sheets of steel roofing, the bolt in the trailer hitch broke and I had to maneuver onto the shoulder with the safety chains holding everything together. That took an hour to fix. To make matters worse, it started to sleet.

After buying the roofing steel, I discovered that the extra-long nails I needed were in short supply. I spent hours going to all the building supply stores in two different towns before I finally found a store with the right-size roofing nails.

I felt thwarted.

October 10

Today I set a goal and achieved it. I finished laying the last of the flooring, and applied the first coat of varnish. It was 40 degrees and rainy, so I probably should have waited, but the long-range forecast is for more of the same, so I went ahead anyway. Then I built a platform under my pump, and bolted it down.

October 11

I spent most of the day working on the floor. First I had to buy more varnish. While I brushed on the final coat, I lit the kerosene heater in the basement. I hope it will warm the place enough for the varnish to dry.

Once the floor was done, I covered my four gable end vents with heavy plastic sheets, and cleaned up the yard a little.

Then I settled down to a delightful campfire. A strong wind has managed to clear away the clouds, but the wind goes right through

The chimney

my parka . . . and leather vest . . . and wool shirt . . . and
sweater . . . and T-shirt . . .

October 12

A light blizzard made working conditions less than desirable. I
built frames for my two skylights, and then was glad to have to
drive the afternoon bus route for Daryl.

When I got home, I faced the fact that for three days it had been
both below freezing and wet, so my sleeping bags were damp from
condensation. Not being able to hang them out for three wet days
led me to the only logical conclusion: Go to Duluth!

October 13

Donna and I returned early from Duluth, and started in on the
south roof.

It was hard, hard, hard. I yelled at the roof, bled on the roof,
and almost cried on the roof.

I used sheets of galvanized steel on the roof, inspired by old
cabins I had come across hidden in the mountains of Wyoming.
The nails bounced on the steel, and I smashed my thumb over and
over again, until it finally occurred to me that I could hold the nails
with a pair of pliers.

In our old persistent, if unprofessional, way, we finished the
side, installed two skylights, and put a coat of wax on my gorgeous
floor.

Later, in Bridgeman's, I ordered a side dish of hot grease.
Rubbing it on, it took most of the roofing tar off my hands, and
gave the waitresses, cooks and manager something to wonder
about.

Moving In

October 14

A day short of six months from the day I moved north, I took down my tent and moved into my cabin. It's far from done, but it's livable.

I slept in my loft for the first time, and through the skylight, looked up at a sky full of clouds. I love it.

Dave finished the chimney while I shifted my things from the tent to the cabin. At 2:00 P.M. I left for Minneapolis. Mother had tickets for us to see Liza Minnelli — a welcome break.

Mother is responsible for my personal cultural enrichment program.

October 19

The roof is nearly done, and my life is filled with a whole new set of tasks. Instead of raising logs and chopping notches, I'm putting up pictures, installing a drain system, hooking up a wood heater, organizing . . .

It was too rainy to finish the roof today, but I worked all day inside just putting more things in order.

Dave said to let the chimney cure for a week, but I've got my great-grandparents' stove ready to go.

Jamie and his friend George are coming to hunt this weekend. I'll go to Duluth so they can have the cabin to themselves, but when I come back, there'll be a fire going, and heat to spare.

October 23

This evening I'm having my first quiet, this-is-how-it's-gonna-be night at home.

It is, and will be, like this: wood I split this afternoon is keeping the air a birch-scented 72 degrees; dishes are drying in a sink I installed today; my kitchen counter and shelves are organized; Tschaikovsky is doing very well on National Public Radio; Lonach, Chisholm and McKay are basking by the heater; and I'm at ease.

The financial picture is less serene. It's bleak.

Savings	$ 1.00
Checking	$79.14
Wallet	$15.46
TOTAL	$95.60 and falling

That's all there is; there isn't any more.

My diet may be limited to potatoes and carrots for a while, but my life is more than full. Mr. Iverson visited today and before he left, said I was well-liked and highly thought of in the community.

He didn't have to tell me that. It's easier not to put a sincere compliment into words. But he took the trouble, and left me feeling warm and welcome.

October 29

As I lay in bed, I watched the Seven Sisters tiptoe acrosss the sky just before it clouded up for a long rain.

October 31

For Halloween, I spent an hour dressing up as a horrible, green-faced, wrinkled old hag. Then I waited to pass out candy to the kids in the area. Nobody came.

Splitting firewood

If I didn't live here, would I walk down a dark drive to a candle-lit log cabin on a stormy Halloween night? No.

I just hope I don't eat all the candy bars at one sitting.

Thanksgiving

November 22

Ralph Waldo Emerson said, "Hospitality consists of a little fire, a little food, and an immense quiet." That's what I keep on hand for my guests — a little fire, a little food, and an immense quiet.

Jamie and Mother came for Thanksgiving dinner. I served only what I produced or gathered myself: potatoes, carrots, wild rice, cattail roots and beet wine.

It was meager by some standards, I suppose, but I believe it was a feast — a reflection of the first Thanksgiving, whose participants had produced a harvest and successfully coped with a merciless wilderness environment.

As I look from my snug cabin at the light snow on the ground and hear the ice tentatively bridging the river, I realize how much I have: a supportive family, caring friends, delightful neighbors, and a dream.

THE FIRST WINTER:

PART TWO

REFLECTIONS IN THE SNOW

Planned Poverty

I am poor. I should be; I spent every penny I had on my cabin, so now in place of money, I have some land and a small home.

Actually, in terms of having what I want, I'm rich. But in terms of money, I'm poor. That's a circumstance I feel good about. Living with little is something I carefully planned before I left my teaching job and the questionable comforts money can buy.

Now I'm well settled into my cabin, and the tease of fall has turned into the no-nonsense of winter.

With my entire wealth folded inside a thin billfold, I am face to face with poverty and winter. Both have come to visit me, and I welcome them as friends.

Reflections in the Snow

Winter is a special time in northern Minnesota. It's harsh, powerful, serene and beautiful. These adjectives are very meaningful to me, living alone in the woods. My primitive home keeps me close to the essence of those adjectives.

After the day's wood is split, and I've hauled it in by the stove, I spend happy moments by a freshly stoked fire, reflecting on my experiences of winter, my experiences of being poor, my experiences of being poor this first winter in my new home

My Great-Grandparents Stove

My great-grandparents on my mother's side lived in Carlton County, about sixty miles east of my place. They had a small box stove that held about three small logs at the most.

The stove heats my single room now, but I can't say it does a terrific job of it. Oh, it's charming, with its scroll work in the cast iron, but it's so tiny it doesn't hold a fire very long. I'm accustomed to being able to see my breath when I'm inside my cabin.

When I get home from work, I leave my hat and jacket on, build a fresh fire, and sit as close to the stove as I can get. Soon my knees begin to scorch and I back off. Later the hat and jacket come off. I squeeze another log into the firebox, and climb up to the sleeping loft.

The scene is similar each morning, but I have the added task of breaking up the ice on the dog's water dish. In my cabin, it's in the mid-twenties; outside, it's usually considerably colder.

During severe cold stretches, with temperatures stubbornly remaining way below zero, I sometimes get tired of the frozen floor and frosty air, and set the alarm clock to go off every two hours throughout the night. Each obnoxious mid-dream ring brings me down to the stove to fire it up. If I decide to sleep through it, and let the house drop to 20 degrees or so, the oil in the clock jells, eliminating the alarm option.

At such times, with the clock stuck at 4:00 A.M., and the oatmeal freezing to the spoon as I eat, I crave the luxury of waking up or coming home from work to a warm house. I know I left a lot of luxuries behind when I chose to move north, but Thoreau's cabin was warm at night, wasn't it?

The Cold Engine

A garage is something I plan to build in a year or two. In the meantime, I have a 1974 pickup truck, with 115,000 miles on it, that doesn't like to start between November and April.

Lacking electricity to plug in an engine heater, I've solved the problem in two steps. First, I built a strange, sloping shelter of hay bales that encloses most of the truck and breaks the wind. The second step is only necessary on sub-zero days. A half-hour prior to departure time, I fill an open metal tool box with coals from the fire and slide it under the engine. My truck starts as well as it does in mid-summer.

One side of me finds that victory very gratifying, but another side of me wishes that cars had never been invented. I tend to express my disapproval of certain things by abstaining from the use of those things. For example, I don't use meat or electricity, to protest the industries they represent.

I don't like the oil industry in particular, or the whole industrial revolution in general. In addition to the obvious environmental damage, I worry about the effect of all kinds of automation on American values and priorities.

Nevertheless, I have a truck. Faced again with the principle of expediency, I use the truck almost every day. It's my compromise with the twentieth century.

Snap, Crackle, Pop

I lie in bed some nights and listen to the cold.

The sap freezing in the trees will expand and crack the wood. It sounds like a gunshot if it's close. Silence follows, until more trees crack and pop.

My cabin logs are still a little green. I wake up with a jolt when one of them pops from the cold, and the loft jars underneath me. I wonder if the roof has split loose from the ridgepole, and then fall back asleep.

Ninety Degrees in the Shade

My new woodstove finally arrived. Made by Vermont Castings, it's a beautiful stove. It's styled like a Franklin, with doors that open, but the fire burns long and hot when it's closed up.

I suddenly find myself living on a tropical island in the dead of a Minnesota February.

Now my loft hits 90 degrees, and I throw open the window for a refreshing gulp or two of winter breeze. It surprises me each time I get home from work and open the door to a comfortable temperature.

Life seems very easy.

Chinking

There's no permanent chinking between my logs yet. Until the walls have thoroughly dried and settled, there's no point in chinking, because it would just crack and crumble as the house shrinks down.

As a temporary measure I've got fiberglass stuffed between the logs, and strips of lath nailed over that. In a year I'll chink with

cement right on top of the lath, inside and out. Until then, I live with an inside wind-chill factor.

Since my new heater came, I relish each draft, and often sit in the breeziest place I can.

The Outhouse

Seventy-five feet south of my cabin there's a bit of a clearing off to the right. That's where the outhouse sits.

It's a pleasant walk, day or night, warm or cold. I especially enjoy a late night look at the stars.

But is it uncomfortable to actually use an outdoor john at 20 below? Heavens, no. I installed a styrofoam seat, which provides instant heat on contact.

That may seem like a peculiar detail to mention, to those who use indoor facilities year-round, but for one who steps outside to answer nature's call, it's a detail that makes nature much nicer.

Cleanliness

It's been said that cleanliness is next to Godliness. Whoever is responsible for that statement certainly never lived without plumbing in northern Minnesota.

It's not that I don't make an effort, but the all-American daily shower is simply out of the question.

I strongly suspect that the daily shower concept was unheard of prior to the days of mass communication and multi-million-dollar advertising campaigns.

Once enough homes had television sets, and a majority of Americans were subjected to daily viewings of lovely bodies lathering up for thirty seconds of hygienic bliss, it was only a matter of time before bathing became a national pastime.

Now I'm all in favor of hygiene, but I don't have a shower, so I rely on older methods.

In the summer I can be as squeaky clean as any shower fanatic. I just jump in the river and scrub.

From October through April, I use the traditional sponge-bath system. I heat a bucket of water on the stove, pour it in a pan, and wash. It's simple and effective, and I do it often.

(I discovered that the old bathtub I worked so hard to get is entirely impractical. A gallon of water right next to a hot stove is infinitely more pleasant than spending hours pumping and heating enough water to fill the tub. Now the tub is in storage, and in its place I built two guest bunks.)

I must admit that when I visit friends or family, I do enjoy the all-American shower.

Winter bathing facility

The Sweat Lodge

After reading about the Cree Indians' "sweet houses," I decided to build my own sweat lodge (an Indian sauna). My sweat lodge looks like a tipi, but it's different in several ways.

Two friends and I put it up in a few days. I wanted it to be stiff, so we soaked the cloth in glue. It was like a giant paper-mâché sculpture, using cloth instead of paper. When about two-thirds of the lodge was done, I had used up all the cloth I had bought, so I ran into the cabin and took every sheet I owned, including the one on my bed, and sacrificed them all to the glue pot. Once the structure dried, I coated it with tar and a final coat of light brown roof coating. It's stiff and totally windproof. Inside is my great-grandparents' wood heater, which I covered with rocks.

The first time I used the sweat lodge, I built a roaring fire in the stove and waited for the rocks to heat up so the steam bath could begin. Four hours later, I was still waiting. The temperature inside the tipi rose steadily, but at a very slow rate. Finally, my patience dwindled, and I couldn't wait any longer.

I stood naked in the middle of the pitch-black tipi. Splashing a little water on the hot rocks, I could hear it turn to steam. I didn't sweat. I couldn't sweat. It wasn't hot enough to sweat. Retreating to my cabin, I decided that the next time I used the sweat lodge, I would have to allow more time for the fire to heat the air.

The second time I fired up the sweat lodge stove, a strong north wind created a down draft in the stovepipe. Nothing I tried would make the smoke go up and out. It poured relentlessly into the tipi.

Time after time, I held my breath and charged through the door to stoke the fire and adjust the draft. The smoke burned my eyes. When I finally accepted my defeat, I realized that I smelled like a piece of smoked salmon.

Now my tipi is a handy storage area. Every time I look at it, I am grateful for the bucket of hot water that sits on the stove in my cabin.

The Sun

My cabin has two skylights, one over my bed in the loft, and the other centered over the room.

The winter sun never gets much higher than the trees, and its path of light is long and nearly horizontal. A shaft of sun pours through the centered skylight, forming a rectangle of light on the chimney, right up by the ceiling.

As the days get longer and the sun climbs in the sky, the rectangle inches down the chimney. By June the light will shine on the floor, almost directly below the skylight.

It's like a seasonal sundial, advertising the nearing of spring.

Bruno's Truck Stop

I work six hours a day at Bruno's truck stop. My office is a six-by eight-foot camper trailer. Truckers who use the self-service pumps come in and pay me for their fuel. It's not an overly demanding job. The advantage of it is the time it gives me to write.

I earn as little as they can legally pay, and it's just enough. My weekly check covers a little food, gas for the pickup, and a small assortment of bills. It doesn't cover extras like travel, car trouble, medical costs, clothes, or whatever else people spend money on.

My existence is hand-to-mouth, and one free meal a day at the truck stop keeps me alive and healthy.

I've formed a new opinion of truck drivers since working at Bruno's. I used to think of them as obsessed maniacs, delighting in forcing four-cylinder vehicles onto the shoulder, seeking out treacherous mountain routes when their air brakes were losing pressure, and eager to take a run at twelve-foot bridge clearances.

The drivers I've gotten to know are family men who work long hours day after day, paying better than five hundred dollars a week for fuel, just to keep on the road.

They spend hours, days, even up to two weeks parked in a line of trucks, waiting to dump a load of grain.

They worry about their weight, because a bag of Baby Ruths helps ease the monotony on the road.

When I see these drivers at Bruno's, every one of them has a smile and joke or a good word for me.

Now when a truck doesn't quite give me the room I'd like on the highway, I look to see who the maniac is, and wave as he sails by.

Why?

I've been asked why I choose poverty. Not everyone understands how I could leave the security of a teaching job to live alone in a tiny cabin, in an area where jobs are scarce and often temporary.

Actually, I never chose to be poor. My choice was to build a cabin in northern Minnesota. I realized that poverty would almost certainly be a consequence of that choice.

There are many days when my resources dwindle to some loose change and a can or two of soup. Then I look around. I'm sitting in a comfortable home I've dreamed of all my life. It's all paid for. Just outside the door are eight acres of woods and the Mississippi River. The setting is tranquil and welcoming.

I'm living just the way I've always wanted to live. This gives me a real sense of personal freedom. It required some scrimping and saving to get here, but now that I'm here, money has very little to do with my way of living.

Recently I was asked what changes I would make if I was suddenly blessed with a windfall of money. I honestly don't think I would change anything. I certainly wouldn't move, install electricity and buy a television set, or put a toilet in the house.

I might eat a little better.

Engine Trouble

Christmas marked the beginning of the engine trouble season.

Santa brought me a broken carburetor, a plugged radiator, a leaky water pump, a cracked battery, and a dead alternator and regulator.

I've learned that if anything is going to go wrong with a vehicle, it will go wrong out of town, after dark, during the nastiest cold snap.

That in itself is acceptable, but the repairs brought me to the low point of having to borrow money from a friend. I paid it back promptly, but the situation illustrates one of the main drawbacks of being poor. On a survival basis, things can go along just fine. But when unexpected expenses come along, there's no safety net.

Daily Bread

I put my yellow mixing dish on the counter. Then I add a half cup of whole-wheat flour, some powdered milk, a little scoop of oatmeal, a fistful of bran, a dash of salt and about a tablespoon of baking powder. I add to that a little real maple syrup, a lump of shortening and enough water to make a thick paste. It looks revolting.

I dump the glop into a cast iron frying pan, and fry it over coals, tipping the pan on its side for the last few minutes to brown the top. When it's golden-brown and cooked through, I spread butter on top, put my feet up, and chew, chew, chew. It's my version of bannock, a very old way of making bread, used by Indians, trappers and voyageurs of the Northland.

It's a heavy, filling, nourishing bread — the staple of my diet. I supplement it with fruit, soup, beans and nuts. I lack imagination for low-budget cooking, so I tend to stick with a few favorites. It may sound like an appalling diet, but I thrive on it, and I love it.

The only time I've been sick in two years was a bout with food poisoning after eating in a nice restaurant for a treat.

Firewood

I buy firewood in loggers' cords: eight-foot lengths, piled in a stack that measures four feet high and four feet wide. I always cut some wood from my own property, but I find the task of carrying logs as heavy as me up and down the steep hills by my house more than I want to tackle. Firewood purchased in loggers' cords is fairly inexpensive in northern Minnesota, so the time and effort it saves me is worth every penny. The fun begins when the logs are dropped off a flatbed truck beside my cabin. Friends are extra precious at such a time.

My small chain saw struggles admirably to cut the logs into stove-length bolts. Stooping with a chain saw for hours is a curse on my back, and I rest by switching to a peavey to sort and separate the logs.

Splitting is the most satisfying part of the firewood process. Each clean split is a victory and a noble act. A piece of heat conquered. Birch, maple and oak are easily conquered, but the battle rages long with elm. I've fought as long as half an hour with a stubborn piece of elm, and my victory is tainted with vengeance when I finally pull it apart. After the splitting comes the tedium of stacking the wood so it can air-dry for a year before I burn it.

A fire is a source of pleasure all its own. Sitting beside a purring wood stove is like basking in the sun; the warmth penetrates and soothes. The callouses on my hands and the firmness of my arms remind me of my victory over the woodpile.

Fun

The woods are my own private Disneyland. When I feel like being entertained, I put on the cross-country skis and explore the shore of the river. I'm gradually making a more definite trail to cut down on the obstacles.

My husky loves to ski with me. She squirms impatiently while I buckle on her harness, and when I grab the reins, she takes off like an F-15. McKay flies over the trail with me while I call "Gee," and "Haw," imagining that she's obeying my directions.

At home, I amuse myself with either a pencil or guitar in hand. I work on an assortment of plays, books and children's stories, and compose songs as they occur to me. At the piano, I sing a repetoire

that ranges from the complete works of Gershwin, to World War II tearjerkers, to traditional Scottish folk songs, depending on my mood.

Extra Cash

There are days when the auto insurance, rabies shots, real estate tax and snow tire bills all seem to come due at once. The truck stop check can't stretch far enough to accommodate them, or alleviate my panic.

Extra cash is the only answer, and I earn it by tuning pianos, substitute teaching, and cleaning chimneys.

The most recent financial emergency sent me to an isolated farm in my chimney sweep's top hat and tails. At the top of the two-story frame house, I encountered a totally plugged chimney and a stiff, sub-zero wind.

For two hours I chiseled at the tarry plug, until the chimney finally had a draft. Meanwhile, the twenty-mile-an-hour draft had turned my fingers into popsicles, and I was grateful to get back to the home fire, cash in pocket.

I thought that was hard-earned money until I was called to substitute for an elementary school physical education teacher.

The schedule called for me to supervise eleven classes during the day. I started each class with some warm-up calesthenics, and made the near-fatal error of leading the exercises by doing them along with the children.

For two days I suffered the consequences of one hundred and ten push-ups, sit-ups and toe-touches.

Gold

Sometimes people pay me in gold for cleaning their chimneys. I know it's gold, but superficially, it has the appearance of a small pile of firewood.

Luxury

All my life I've been unable to adapt to getting up early. In junior high, I repeatedly paid for the problem by being kept after school on detention.

As a teacher, my morning classes always saw the worst side of me.

Now I keep the schedule that is natural for me. I go to bed late, when I'm tired, and I wake up when I'm through sleeping. Bells don't ring, the radio doesn't play, and no one blows reveille. I wake up peacefully and slowly, with the sun shining on me through the skylight above my bed.

It's a small luxury, but one I cherish. It makes me really glad to be where I am.

Winter Camping

For a change of pace and a little adventure, a winter camping trip can be the highlight of a long winter. The daily routine is basically simple:

1. Load a small and a large fiberfill mummy bag, a closed-cell foam pad, and some high-energy food into a backpack.
2. Ski to a secluded spot under some virgin pines and set up a well-ventilated tent.
3. Dress down to a light sweater and saw up dead wood until dark.
4. Put on a wool hat, extra sweater, wool shirt, down vest, down or fiberfill parka, wind shirt and pants, and enjoy a hot meal by the fire.
5. Change into fresh wool underwear, put the small sleeping bag inside the large sleeping bag, and crawl into the former.
6. Practice the crawl stroke or shadow box vigorously for sixty seconds, and sleep well.

There are wolf tracks to be seen while winter camping. Waterfalls stand frozen in rugged, abstract sculptures. In remote stands of pine, the snow is deep and clean. If you camp far enough away from snowmobile trails, the only sounds you hear are the wind and the shoosh of your own skis.

The lack of insects and the fact that few species of birds stay north make the winter woods a place of incredible peace. Just as people speak in hushed voices in the great cathedrals of Europe, I tend to speak softly when I winter camp.

I always return from one of these camping trips with a new respect for winter.

Unnecessary Necessities

I do without a refrigerator. In the winter, my porch serves the purpose, and in the summer I just don't buy perishables. Powdered milk is adequate.

My cabin is lit with a kerosene lamp. Fifty years ago, twenty-five per cent of the population did the same.

In another fifty years, the earth may wish we had all done the same.

I don't have a stove with hot plates and an oven, but the surface of my woodstove cooks my food with an even heat, and I often bake in the coals. The same woodstove takes the place of a gas or oil-burning furnace.

My cabin has no faucets with running water. Two steps from my porch, I have a large hand pump. Sometimes I use it directly, and other times I pump twenty gallons into a hose that leads to a holding tank in the cellar. From there I can pump it right into the sink with a small cistern pump. I have water to spare.

My plumbing system is simple. A short drain takes water from my sink to a bucket, and my outhouse is maintenance-free. The pipes don't freeze, and I never pay a plumber.

I've found that a checkbook is unnecessary. My income, expenses and mathematical ability are all so low that it doesn't pay to try to balance an account and put up with monthly service charges. I handle my finances with the old stand-by: cash.

Essentially, the so-called necessities I do without all have easy substitutes.

Necessary Necessities

There are a few things I haven't found substitutes for, and I wouldn't want to.

I have a phone to stay in touch with my family and close friends. I cringe at the bill each month, but there's always a piano that needs tuning.

Mail is another necessity, another way I stay in touch with people.

Books, news magazines and the radio keep me in touch with the world, and I wouldn't be without them.

Movies sometimes diappoint me, but I don't let that bother me, and see one when I can.

During the worst years of the Depression, radio, movies and bookmobiles all flourished, so I know I'm not the only poor person to consider such things necessities. Of course, they're not really necessary, but they add lightness, and color, and stimulation to a day.

Pure, unadorned survival can be an interesting challenge on wilderness trips, but for year-round living there are people, places, and events that I want to enjoy.

New Year's Eve

I like New Year's Eve celebrations to be unique.
In college, I camped alone in a desert.

Several years in a row I camped out on the Canadian border.
One year I attended a nun's birthday party in a convent.
Next year, I'll sleep in my tipi.

I like to be creative on New Year's Eve. When others try to recall their hazy memories of an 80-proof party, I like to know that I had a small adventure, with each detail intact in my mind.

Break–up

Towards spring, the ice on the river starts to groan and the snow turns to mush. My skis sink and leave wet, black tracks. I stay close to shore.

In early April, the ice melts away as the current washes the thaw downstream. The shore ice cracks and rumbles, and joins the other ice barges migrating towards New Orleans.

By May, the river is quiet, and overflows its banks. The temperature hits sixty, and I trade my skis for canoe and bicycle.

Winter seems to be gone forever, and I miss my frozen friend.

Epilogue

My first winter is over; I swam and gardened and luxuriated through another summer, and now another winter is on my threshold.

Meanwhile, a new dream is beginning to take shape. My eyes are focused on the north, and my notebook is filling up with plans for a canoe trip to Hudson Bay.

It's a new challenge to plan for, and I anticipate new hardships, new difficulties, and new frustrations. I also anticipate new growth, new learning, new dimensions of my own character.

So, I'm off in pursuit of a new dream, and as others occur to me, I'll pursue them too. I'll "step to the music that I hear, however measured or far away."

Glossary

1. **Boom:** One or two poles suspended at a 45-degree angle from a stationary pole. Used for lifting heavy objects.
2. **Cant hook:** Provides leverage to roll and shift logs around. Generally, a cant hook can.
3. **Chain saw:** A noisy, undependable machine.
4. **Chinking:** Material stuffed between logs to seal gaps and prevent drafts.
5. **Chisholm:** A Siamese cat who looks in a mirror and sees a lion.
6. **Come-a-long:** Tongs with a long handle, enabling two or more people to drag a log.
7. **Draw knife:** A two-handled knife used for peeling logs.
8. **Gin pole:** A synonym for Boom.
9. **Lonach:** A Siamese cat who looks in a mirror and sees W.C. Fields.
10. **McKay:** A husky-wolf mix who enjoys cheese for supper and Siamese cats for dessert.
11. **Peavey:** A synonym for cant hook.
12. **Scribe:** A large compass used to mark the outline of a notch.
13. **Shears:** Two vertical poles, lashed at the top to form an "A" — used for lifting heavy objects.
14. **Tongs:** A heavy iron claw that grips logs.

About the Author

Born in 1950, Laurie Shepherd began canoeing and camping as a small child. In her teens, she attended the Minnesota Outward Bound School, and as a young adult, she expanded her outdoor activities to include winter camping, backpacking and mountain climbing. She has taught orienteering and rock climbing, as well as canoeing.

A graduate of the University of Minnesota, she was an art teacher for several years. She has also been a school-bus driver, restaurant cook, piano tuner and chimney sweep. She has written several plays, and composes music.

She is currently a special education teacher and track coach in a small town near her log-cabin home in northern Minnesota.